EVEN MORE
FIVE-MINUTE
MYSTERIES

Also available in this series

Five-Minute Mysteries
More Five-Minute Mysteries
Further Five-Minute Mysteries

EVEN MORE
FIVE-MINUTE
MYSTERIES

40 New Cases
of Murder and Mayhem
for You to Solve

Ken Weber

© 1996 by K.J. Weber Limited

Printed in [TK]

9   8   7   6   5   4   3   2   1
Digit on the right indicates the number of this printing

Library of Congress Cataloging-in-Publication Number 96-67154

ISBN 1-56138-745-2

Designed and produced by
Stoddart Publishing Co. Limited
34 Lesmill Road
Toronto, Canada
M3B 2T6

Cover design by Frances J. Soo Ping Chow
Cover illustration © Sandra Dionisi/SIS
Typeset by Tannice Goddard

This book may be ordered by mail from the publisher.
Please include $2.50 for postage and handling.
But try your bookstore first!

Running Press Book Publishers
125 South Twenty-second Street
Philadelphia, Pennsylvania 19103-4399

*With thanks to 9J,
for that's how all this started*

Contents

EVEN MORE
FIVE-MINUTE
MYSTERIES

1

The Body on
Blanchard Beach

LIKE THE OTHERS SITTING ON THE SIDE facing the window, Sue Cremer pulled her chair closer to the table as soon as K. D. Lapp came in. Everyone did it automatically and almost at the same time, a habit they'd developed because K. D. always whipped his crutches forward one after the other in a wide half-circle, and he needed extra room to get by.

As her boss settled in at the head of the long table, it occurred to Sue that she might have lost her carefully planned advantage in the pull forward. This afternoon's meeting was about the body found on Blanchard Beach earlier in the day. There would be slides projected at the wall across from K. D. Lapp, slides of the site and — the reason Sue Cremer had got her usual early seat — slides of the murdered body.

For two years as director of Information Services in the office of the county coroner, she had successfully avoided ever looking at a dead body, either the real thing or even a picture. It was a secret she'd kept from her colleagues all this time by doing things like sitting third chair from the end on Chief Coroner Lapp's right. That strategy ensured she would always have the obsessive Doctor Reuven Shallmar immediately beside her, blocking her view of the screen. Shallmar was a brilliant pathologist whose forensic skills were almost as legendary as the tantrums he threw whenever his notions of order and sequence were disturbed. One of those notions was that he had the right, always and absolutely without exception, to sit in the same place at every staff meeting. No one opposed him.

The man's wishes and his peculiar behavior made no difference whatever to Sue. What mattered to her was Shallmar's abnormally large head, made even larger by a sunburst of crinkly red hair. She had learned through practice that by sitting just so, she could appear to be gazing intently at the screen when in fact her line of sight was entirely obscured by the pathologist's mighty skull.

When the call came down for today's meeting she had, as usual, positioned herself with time to spare, for this was going to be a bad one. In the past six months two bodies had been found on Blanchard Beach, at different times but less than a kilometer apart. Both had been adult females and both had been mutilated after death. Whoever was responsible was a very sick person. The tabloid press was already ranting about a serial killer and the more responsible media was on the brink of joining the chorus. This morning's discovery of a third body was sure to tip them over the edge. That's why, in every office around the city that was even remotely connected to law enforcement, there had been meetings like this going on all day.

Chief Coroner Lapp rapped his knuckles for attention.

"All right, people. Let's get on task here. I'm leaving for the police commissioner's office in thirty minutes and I want to be able to take something with me from this meeting. Now the slides we have here are — Ah! Dexter. Thank you for coming."

The door had opened after a single knock. A short black man moved along the wall to an extra chair between Lapp and the window. He wore jeans and a faded T-shirt that loudly proclaimed "No Sweat, Mon!" over an oasis of sand and waving palms.

Lapp introduced him. "I'm not sure all of you know Dexter Treble. These are his photographs we're about to look at and I've asked him to narrate." He lowered his voice slightly. "Can we get going on this right away, Dexter? I'm due at the commissioner's task force and . . ." He let his sentence drift away while Dexter Treble beamed a smile in return.

Dexter acknowledged Lapp's request: "Of course!" Contrary to the initial impression his appearance may have created with some at the table, Dexter was efficient, articulate, and possessed of a crisp British accent.

"Of course," he repeated, and picked up the remote control, turning on the slide projector in the same fluid motion. "It would be helpful if someone could dim the, ah, thank you.

"The first photograph here," — Dexter clicked a slide into position on the carousel — "is of the pertinent section of the area known as Blanchard Beach. It's not my work. This is from the county files. It was taken by the pollution control group about a year ago. No particular significance to our work here other than I thought it would be germane for you to be reminded of what Blanchard Beach looks like when it's not famous, or rather, infamous."

Sue edged forward slightly to see around Reuven Shallmar's bobbing mane. The photograph was a safe one and she had been in the beach area only once before. Blanchard was a lonely stretch about ten minutes' drive from the edge of the city. The beach itself, between the sand dunes and the water, was flat and sandy, but swimming was banned because of a fierce undertow. It was a lonely place most of the time. Even teenagers chose other spots to drag race and carry on. An ideal place to dump things. Sue was leaning forward intently when Dexter Treble clicked in the next slide without warning. Her stomach lurched but then calmed. The shot was innocuous enough. It was a body wrapped in something brown.

"This is taken from a dune looking down on the site. One of mine." Dexter carried on smoothly. "According to the couple that discovered the body, this is exactly what they saw when they came upon it. As you can see, there is the body, then a single set of tire tracks. A remarkably clean site actually. No footprints, unfortunately, but the tread marks from the tires are quite clear. The police lab is working on those right now."

Dexter Treble popped ahead to a close-up of the tire treads in the sand. They were a perfect set. Sue found herself leaning forward just a bit more as Dexter went back to the previous slide.

"Notice the symmetry too. The investigating officer believes that the vehicle was reversed in and driven out after disposing of the cargo. The body itself was wrapped in that beige tarpaulin just as you see. That's the right hand of the victim protruding ever so slightly. Without the hand it would have been difficult to distinguish the body from other flotsam on the beach, especially from a distance. Now, if there were any doubt about murder, this next slide . . ."

Just in time, Sue slid back to safety behind Doctor Shallmar as Dexter clicked in the slide she'd been dreading, but in that second the door opened without a warning knock. It was one of the young whitecoats from the morgue downstairs. He was excited.

"Cadaver's here, Doctor Lapp."

Reuven Shallmar jumped to his feet. "What I've been waiting for!" He turned to the door, then stopped heron-like on one leg and looked back to K. D. Lapp. "Kirk?"

K. D. Lapp waved him on. "Yes, by all means. Call me at the commissioner's office in one hour, no matter what."

Shallmar was released into flight before Lapp even finished speaking. Almost without warning, Sue Cremer's protective barrier had disappeared!

Later that evening she was unable to explain, even to herself, how she'd carried it off, but the instant Doctor Shallmar slammed the door she turned away from the screen to face her boss.

"Doctor Lapp," she said calmly, "could we return to the previous slide, please?"

He looked at her with mild curiosity. Sue almost never spoke at these meetings. Lapp nodded to Dexter, who immediately returned to the close-up of the tire tracks.

"No, sorry. The one before that," Sue insisted.

Dexter accommodated. By now everyone was staring at Sue instead of the screen. More dramatically than was her style, she swept her arm along the table and then pointed at the screen.

"Do you know, Dr. Lapp," she began to wave her finger at the screen in remonstrating fashion, "do you know whether the search for a vehicle has concentrated on a van, by any chance?"

K. D. Lapp peered at Sue and then looked back at the screen.

"By Jove," he said. Then louder. "By Jove!" He grabbed at his crutches. "I don't believe so, not to my knowledge! I don't believe so! By Jove!"

He caught his crutches on the edge of his chair and they clattered to the floor. "Drat!" he shouted at them.

Sue rose to her feet quickly. "I'll go do the telephoning, sir. You're needed here anyway."

Without waiting for an answer, Sue Cremer got to her feet and exited the room, being careful not to look at the screen just in case Dexter Treble decided to move ahead before she was ready.

Sue Cremer has successfully extricated herself from the meeting and at the same time provided what may be a valuable clue. Why does she believe the body was brought to Blanchard Beach in a van?

2

Esty Wills Prepares
for a Business Trip

THE ELEVATOR WAS AGONIZINGLY SLOW. It was overheated too, and smelly, filled with the odor of institutional cleanser and cooking smells, which provided an unwelcome and unasked-for accounting of who had what for dinner the previous night. Still, it gave Sean Hennigar a twinge of mildly vindictive pleasure. All things being equal, the apartment was a dump, a major comedown in lifestyle for Esty Wills — Mr. Flash, as he was called in the D.A.'s office.

Sean moved to lean against the back wall but then thought better of it. No point in having the graffiti come off on his overcoat. Certainly he wanted no souvenir of a visit to Esty Wills, even if the visit was part of his job. Sean was a parole officer, working out of the D.A.'s office in Market Square. Esty Wills was one of his "files." His least favorite: Wills was a notorious con man, well known in Chicago. Nightclubs knew him as a big spender. Mercedes-Benz and Lexus dealerships vied for his attention. Chi-Vegas Charters automatically bumped passengers to suit his demands, and everyone working for the Blackhawks, Cubs, or Bulls knew his seating preferences.

On the other side of the coin, insurance companies had tagged his name on all their software programs. So had practically every police department in northern Illinois. And although the Consumer Protection Agency had not used Wills's name in a recent flyer to seniors, it was clearly him the group had in mind. To Sean Hennigar, and everyone else in the D.A.'s office for that matter, Esty Wills was nothing but an unrepentant career crook who consumed an entirely disproportionate amount of their time and who, despite his convictions, still seemed to be able to wheedle privileges out of the department.

Take now, for example. Wills was about to leave Chicago for three days on a business trip to Asuncion, a clear violation of the conditions of his parole. He had served only four months of his three-year sentence before being paroled (to no one's surprise) and was already applying for special exemptions. In a classic Wills deal, he had managed to have himself retained by the International Monetary Fund, a partner with the Japanese government in an experimental project investigating the viability of growing mulberry bushes in Paraguay, the ultimate object being the raising of silkworms.

The Banco Nacional de Fomento had leaned on the Japanese representatives, who had leaned on the IMF, who had leaned on an assistant deputy secretary at Commerce in Washington, who had leaned on the Cook County D.A., who promptly signed the permission-to-travel form and then called Sean into his office. Wheels spinning wheels, and now Sean was bringing the form to Wills.

Sean reached out to knock on the door of 14B. He couldn't help noting that somehow Wills had snagged a corner apartment. The door opened immediately to reveal a loudly dressed middle-aged man in standard used-car salesman pose. He was holding a wool sock in one hand.

"Don't they come in pairs?" Sean asked without any preliminary. It took Wills aback, but only for a second.

"Ah!" He smiled beneficently. "My favorite mother hen is

becoming a wit! What next? A song and dance?"

Sean stepped into the apartment without waiting for an invitation. He wasn't smiling. Nor did he take the bait. "Let's get this over with," he said. "Show me your ticket and visa, and I'll give you your passport."

Reading Sean's mood, Wills led the way across the small bachelor suite to where his suitcase sat open on a chesterfield, and extracted the two items requested. Sean looked at the airline ticket very closely. At first, he hardly noticed the discrepancy, distracted as he was by the scarf and gloves labeled L. L. Bean and by the other wool sock. Esty Wills was buying from mail order catalogues, it seemed. A far cry from the personal tailor he'd been used to. This gave Sean an inordinate amount of satisfaction, but only briefly, until the ticket upset him.

"Four days?" He frowned at Wills. "What are you trying to pull here!"

Wills spread his hands in another used-car salesman gesture. "Gimme a break! It's travel time! I got to go via Buenos Aires, and connect there to go back north to Asuncion. Takes almost a day. Same thing coming back. And I need two days there. Look, phone the IMF if you want. Or Washington!"

Sean tossed the ticket at the suitcase, and then very reluctantly followed it with Wills's passport. Without another word, he left the apartment and walked down the hall to where the slow elevator waited for him. All the way down he felt uneasy, bothered by something he couldn't put his finger on. The uneasiness stayed with him through the tiny lobby into the parking lot, where he took a minute to blow a skiff of snow off the windshield and peer into Esty Wills's car.

The used stub of a bus ticket on the front seat said Chicago–St. Louis Return. The thought of Esty Wills traveling by bus should have given Sean some satisfaction. The fact too that the car was a two-year-old Pontiac should have reinforced the feeling. But it didn't. Somehow, Sean couldn't shake the conviction that Esty Wills was not going to Asuncion, but for the life of him, Sean couldn't figure out what had triggered that thought.

The suspicion bothered him even more as he left the parking lot. It wasn't helped, either, when he noticed that the Pontiac was in the choicest parking spot in the lot. "Reserved: 14B" had been painted recently on the little sign on the curb.

What is nagging at Sean Hennigar? Other than the fact that Esty Wills is a known con man, which would make one suspect him in any case, what is it that has twigged Sean's subconscious?

3

The Case of
the Buckle File

BEAVER LIFE
AND CASUALTY INSURANCE COMPANY

1 October 1992

Mr. Ernie Buckle
104 West Fort William Road
Thunder Bay, ON
P8L V1X

Dear Mr. Buckle:

Re: Joint Life Policy BV 297562
Ernie & Audrey Buckle

I have received your letter of 25 September 1992 and the enclosed forms authorizing the addition to your policy of a double indemnity clause for accidental death.

Please note that Mrs. Buckle has not signed Form 22A. Since yours is a joint policy with you and your wife as each other's beneficiary, it is necessary that both of you sign. Accordingly, I am returning Form 22A for her signature.

Further, you have not designated a beneficiary to receive the indemnity should it occur that you and Mrs. Buckle encounter a terminal accidental event together. The funds, if such were to occur, would thus be paid to your respective estates on a 50/50 basis, and would therefore be subject to probate fees and taxation. If this is your wish, you and Mrs. Buckle must initial clause 12 on page 2 of Form 22A. However, should you wish to designate a beneficiary, please enter his/her/their name(s) and address(es) in the space below clause 13 on page 2.

I will hold your cheque until I receive the completed Form 22A, and other instructions on the above matters.

Sincerely,

Christine Cooper

Christine Cooper
Client Services

Oct. 12/92

Beaver Insurance Co

Dear Miss Cooper,
Here is the form with my signature that you asked for.
Sorry I didn't do this before. Ernie usually is the one who
looks after these things. Also, like you said, for ~~beneficiais~~
beneficiary we picked my cousin Reenee Clubek in Gibralter.
Hope this is alright now.

Audie Buckle

BEAVER LIFE
AND CASUALTY INSURANCE COMPANY

12 November 1992

Mr. Ernie Buckle
Mrs. Audrey Buckle
104 West Fort William Road
Thunder Bay, ON
P8L V1X

Dear Mr. and Mrs. Buckle:

Re: Joint Policy BV 297562

Enclosed please find notice of confirmation regarding changes to the above policy, with copies for your files.

The changes are effective as of 15 October 1992.

Sincerely,

Jack Hall for Christine Cooper

Christine Cooper

July 29, 1993

Ms Christine Cooper
Beaver Life and Casualty

BY FAX

Your telephone message of 27/07/93 handed to me this a.m.

Body of Ernie Buckle recovered from Wabakimi Lake at 3:15 p.m., 25/07/93. Coroner has ruled accidental death by drowning. No inquest scheduled.

Search for body of Audrey Buckle terminated this a.m. Overturned canoe located in Wabakimi established as belonging to the Buckles. No further search planned. Status of Audrey Buckle is "presumed dead."

We will have full reports available by 10/08/93. You can get these through usual channels from district headquarters in Thunder Bay.

Constable Allan Longboat
Ontario Provincial Police
Search and Rescue Unit
Sioux Lookout

March 18, '94

To Whom It May Concern,
Beaver Life and Casualty Insurance
7272 Barton Street
Hamilton, Ontario
CANADA

VIA AIR MAIL

Dear Sir or Madam,
I am writing in regard to the deaths of Ernie and Audrey Buckle. As you know, I am the beneficiary named in the life insurance policy they held with your company.

Very shortly I will be moving from Gibralter to a project in east Africa. My new address, effective March 31, '94 will be

c/o Central Postal Station
Box 241
Haile Selassie Blvd.
Nairobi 17
KENYA

It would be helpful if you could tell me when the policy benefit will be issued.

I appreciate your help in this matter.

Sincerely,

Irene Clubek

Irene Clubek

On April 2, 1994, Christine Cooper wrote a memo to her immediate superior stating that one item in particular made her feel that Beaver Life and Casualty was being defrauded in this case, and that the case might also involve a felony. What made her feel that?

4

While Little Harvey
Watched

THE STARLINGS CAME IN EARLY the night before Ollie
Wicksteed was killed. Little Harvey had watched them from
his bedroom window. Black, raucous, a seething, constantly
shifting mass that filled the air with ugly croaking. Usually
they came in just before sunset but that night they were early,
hundreds of them filling up the branches of the old beech
tree behind the house.

Grandpa Bottrell said starlings were bad luck. Two years
ago, in the fall, the first time Little Harvey remembered them
coming in such numbers, Grandpa had taken the old twelve
gauge and fired into the tree. It drove the starlings away, but
not far and not for long. At the peak of the echoing bang they
had risen in an elastic cloud that grew and shrank and shifted
above the tree and then simply pulled itself down on the barn
roof not far away. Five minutes later they were back in the
beech tree and they stayed there, because Momma had taken
the shotgun and hidden it. Momma didn't have much
patience for behavior like that. It was another one of the
things she called "nonsense" (a word she used a lot).

Little Harvey rather agreed with her. The shotgun scared

him. As for the bad luck part, well, that was different. Grandpa Bottrell always seemed to know about that stuff, and even though Momma called it foolish old peoples' talk, the next day Poppa fell off the ladder out by the implement shed. He was laid up a long time and the neighbors had to finish the ploughing.

It was the next year that Grandpa Bottrell got sick. The same week the starlings showed up. Not as many as the year before — at least Momma said so — but still enough to fill up the old beech tree at sunset and make it impossible to hear anybody talk if you were outside unless they shouted right into your ear. What scared Little Harvey so much was that the day they went away for good that year was the day Grandpa died.

Now they were here again. And Harvey no longer had any doubts about the bad luck. He was in the second grade now and for the first time he was really beginning to like school. This year he didn't even mind the long ride every morning on the old yellow bus. Ms. Caswell was the reason. She was just the best teacher. Every day was fun, but now he couldn't go. The day the starlings arrived Little Harvey had got scarlet fever and he had to stay home. Nobody gets scarlet fever these days, Momma had said to Doctor Sannalchuk, and what about the vaccinations when he was a baby? And Doctor Sannalchuk said there were always a very few kids in whom the vaccines didn't "take." Little Harvey had to be one of those. Just bad luck. So he had spent most of a week in his room.

At first he didn't mind, because he was so sick. But by the time Ollie Wicksteed was killed, Little Harvey had felt more like doing things and the starlings at least gave him something to watch. That's why he was looking out the window when Ollie was crushed by the big beech tree. Harvey's room was the only one that faced the back yard.

At the funeral folks said it was an accident and maybe even a blessing seeing as how Ollie gave his brother such trouble all these years and wasn't really good for anything. Harvey listened to the talk outside the church and he wasn't exactly sure what they meant by "good for anything," but he had a feeling it was because Ollie was funny in the head. People called him retarded but there was a girl in Ollie's class in school who everybody said was retarded and she didn't act the way Ollie did.

Ollie's brother, Carson, was always having to take things out of Ollie's mouth. Once Little Harvey had overheard Poppa say that Carson had had to pull Ollie out of the manure pile at the south barn because he'd tried to burrow in like a groundhog.

"Shame what Carson's had to do for that man these years," Poppa had said. "Every minute he's got to watch. And what does he get for it? His wife leaves him, and you can't blame her after what Ollie done to her that time. Carson, he can't go nowhere. Can't even do a decent day's work. Not much money in firewood no more anyway but a man's got to work. No wonder Carson drinks so heavy."

Momma's response was muffled but Little Harvey was sure he'd heard her mention the special home where Ollie had lived for a time and where he got kicked out and they wouldn't take him back. It was something about a girl there but Harvey didn't know for sure what it was because every time the grown-ups talked about it, they changed the subject when he came near.

It was not only because of the scarlet fever that Harvey was watching from the bedroom window when Carson came over to cut up the beech tree. It was because he was afraid of Ollie. He didn't used to be, but then Momma had said, "Now the Wicksteed's are neighbors and I don't like to tell you this but you stay away from that Ollie. Don't you dare ever let me catch you makin' fun of him but you stay away."

That's why Little Harvey watched from the safety of the second floor. The night before, a big wind had toppled the old beech, torn it out roots and all, so that it lay tipped on its side like a giant that had fallen with its feet in the air. The hole left by the roots was wide, but because of the way beech trees grow it was shallow, and when Ollie stood upright in it his head was above the surface of the ground. Harvey had watched him rest his chin on the rim of the hole and lick the stones where one edge of the root system still clung to the ground. Then he'd seen Carson turn off the chain saw up at the other end of the tree and throw it down by the branches he'd just cut off and come over and swear at Ollie and kick away the stones. Ollie just sat in the hole for a while after that, but before long he got up onto his knees and began scooping out a burrow with his hands, putting the sandy ground in the pockets of his overalls. That's what he was doing when the stump came down on top of him.

That night the starlings came back at sunset, but they were confused because the beech tree wasn't there. They hovered where the branches used to be as if waiting for them to return, shifting and floating and diving the way they always did. What Little Harvey noticed most of all was how quiet they were. It was as though they knew something. That bothered him a great deal. He knew something too, something about Ollie and the way he died. But who should he tell? And how should he explain it?

It would seem that Little Harvey doesn't accept the idea that Ollie Wicksteed's death was an accident. Why has he cause to be suspicious?

5

The Murder of
Mr. Norbert Gray

JIM LATIMER HUNG UP THE PHONE. "That was F.A.R.,"
he said.

From his desk across the overcrowded squad room, Mike
Roslin nodded absently. He was staring at an open evidence
bag.

"Thought so," he acknowledged finally. "And don't tell me.
The Beretta's hers, right?"

"Uh huh." Jim Latimer nodded. "Registered in 1984, uh,
let's see, on March fifteenth. No, the sixteenth. Firearm
Registration's got data on disk back to 1986. Anything before
that they gotta dig out by hand. That's what took 'em so long
to call back."

Mike Roslin rubbed his elbow back and forth along the
arm of his chair. "And the Luger?" he asked, picking a deadly
looking weapon out of a holster that bore the double light-
ning bolts of the SS on the cover flap.

"His. Registered the same day. They bought both guns at
Intutus Firearms Shop on Mount Pleasant. Luger's registered
for range use. The Beretta can be carried."

"Humpf." Mike was clearly unimpressed. He began to

invert the evidence bag over his desk.

"Wait!" His partner shouted so loud that the two other detectives in the room rose out of their chairs. "You know what happened the last time we used your desk!"

The others chuckled and went back to their work. Mike Roslin had a reputation as the best problem-solver on the homicide squad, but one whose desk, locker, car, and apartment were so covered in flotsam that even he no longer knew what he owned.

"Here," Jim directed. "Dump it on my desk. Then at least we'll know which murder we're trying to solve."

Without a word, Mike carried the bag around to his partner's desk and slowly eased the contents onto the surface. Except for the Luger and its holster, both nestled in the pile of incomplete reports, empty coffee cups, and Mr. Submarine wrappers on Mike's desk, the story of Norbert Gray's untimely demise now lay spread out on Detective Jim Latimer's desk blotter.

Just forty-eight hours ago, Norbert Gray had been shot in the back of the head while sitting at the solid oak rolltop in his den. After an acrimonious and very public divorce from his wife of seventeen years, Gray had been living alone in their custom-built log home in the exclusive Pines district. The ex-wife, Aleyna, was in custody, but not yet formally charged.

There had been one shot at close range from a 9 mm Beretta. Apparently, the shooter — the evidence pointed overwhelmingly at this being the former Mrs. Gray — had stood behind the victim, fired once, and then threw the gun out the balcony doors. It had skidded down the side of the ravine that backed onto the Gray home, and came to rest (lucky for the investigators) against a tree trunk at the edge of a bike path. The techs had quickly determined that the Beretta was indeed the murder weapon, and that it had a single fingerprint on it. At the end of the barrel, curiously, but a clear print nevertheless. More to the point, the print belonged to Aleyna Gray.

The Beretta lay in the center of the pile on Jim Latimer's desk. Mike stuck the eraser end of a pencil inside the trigger guard and absently spun the little gun in circles.

"Something really stinks about all this," he said.

"Yeah," Jim nodded. "You said that yesterday. And this morning too."

"Well, it does," came the reply. "I don't like these near-smoking-gun cases."

This time it was Jim who used a pencil to play with the evidence. "Yeah, but . . ." He stuck the point under an envelope and flipped it over so that Norbert Gray's name and address looked up at them. "There's two of these letters," he said. "Both from her. The one from two weeks ago tells him what a jerk he is, how inadequate he is, what a lousy father, worse as a husband. Sure glad I never had to tangle with this woman. The second one, it's what? Three days before the murder? Tells him what she'd like to do to him."

"Okay, but . . ." Mike took the pencil out of the Beretta's trigger guard and tapped the postal mark and then the stamp on first one letter, then the other. "Personal letters, sure. But everything's typed. WordPerfect, I'd say, and a laser printer. Lots of those around."

"Then what about the will?" Jim asked. Norbert Gray's will had been found on the surface of the rolltop. A line had been drawn through the clauses relating to Aleyna, but there was no signature or initialing near it.

"Sure, what about it? Watch this." Jim winced in disbelief as Mike drew a line across a report lying on Jim's typewriter. "Doesn't tell us a thing!" Mike continued.

"And the cigarettes?" Jim asked the question in almost a whisper. He was still staring at the report.

"Easy to set up. He didn't smoke. She does." Mike pointed a finger at a half-empty pack on the desk. "Yes, it's her brand. Yes, her prints are on the pack, but look, this is garbage. It's all circumstantial."

Jim finally took his eyes off the report. "Still, she sure had motive," he said. "Hated the guy, at least according to the transcript of the divorce. And she's got no alibi: 'I had a cold and took some aspirins and went to bed early.' Pretty weak."

"On the other hand," Mike replied, "we have no eyewitness, and there's really nothing solid here. Look, I'm not on her side, but maybe somebody's setting her up. Maybe somebody's setting *us* up!" He picked up the evidence bag. "All a good lawyer has to do is show that one of these pieces of evidence is phony and the whole lot goes out the window!"

"Yeah." Jim picked up the destroyed report tenderly. "What we need is something like DNA."

Mike looked at his partner. He became so animated that Jim moved to protect his cup of coffee. "That's it!" Mike shouted. We can use DNA to prove one of these pieces of evidence is solid — or phony, for that matter! At least then we'll know if we have a real case or not."

The excitement affected Jim as he too caught the idea. "Yes! DNA!" He reached across the desk, and as he grabbed the evidence bag, a large, grayish-white wad fell out of it. "What's this?" He peered hard at his partner. This wasn't in here before!"

Mike looked perplexed. "Looks like my sock."

"What's it doing in the evidence bag?" Jim asked.

"I dunno."

What, in the evidence the two detectives have, can be subjected to DNA testing?

6

A Holdup at the Adjala Building

IT WAS ONLY 4 P.M. ON A CLEAR MIDSUMMER DAY, but Jeff Ercul expected the street to be in shadows by now. That was yet another reason he had come to deeply regret the transfer from Loretto to the city: urban canyons — long, winding tubes of semi-darkness between rows of skyscrapers.

On this particular stretch of Richmond Street, however, the buildings on the other side were quite a bit shorter than the norm, a tribute to the days when an environmentally sensitive city council had put height restriction bylaws into effect. For that reason, the sun was still lighting up the south and west sides of the Adjala Building, its unique coppery sides and floating design making the kind of grand and lofty statement that prompted even bored frequent fliers to lean over from their aisle seats to get a look.

Jeff squinted as he stood in front of the Adjala Building's main doors. Unlike the outside walls of the building, which were paneled with metal, these were thick plate glass, although they had the same copper tint. It was a glorious building, no question. There was nothing like it in Loretto, where he had spent his first five years on the force. Loretto didn't have live theater either, or big league sports, or the incredible restaurants, or the astounding variety of shopping opportunities. But then, it didn't have crack either, or doors with multiple locks, or people with "subway-elbows," or slums, or beggars on the streets.

The transfer to the city had been offered to Jeff as an avenue to promotion.

"You want to make sergeant," the Human Resources weenie had pointed out to him. You can't sit up there in the boonies for another five years. You gotta get some time where the action is."

Actually, the decision had been easy; Jeff wanted to make sergeant. And the truth was, he really had believed the city would make him feel more like a cop. But the feeling didn't last long. It wasn't just the amount of crime here, and the nature of it. And it wasn't just his disappointment at Twelfth Precinct headquarters. (At first glance, and ever afterwards, it looked to Jeff like a Third World bus station.) Nor was it things like the downtown streets blocking out the sun. He wanted to go back home because, somehow, crime was different there. Not just that there was less of it, and indeed there was much less. Rather, it was more the fact that crime was harder to commit. People watched out for other people. They knew what was going on, and they cared. Here, nobody watched. It was an urban virtue to be isolated from what was going on around you.

Take the theft he was investigating right now, a holdup in broad daylight, just before lunch, right here where he was standing. Not a single witness could be found. Even the victim had not seen the thief.

A courier carrying bearer bonds had felt a gun in her back — an iffy point in Jeff's view; she said it was a gun, but she hadn't seen it, only felt it. The thief had ordered her to stand still and not turn around. Then he'd pulled the strap off her shoulder and over her head, taking her delivery bag.

"Then he says . . . he says . . ." This had all been reported to

Jeff through an enormous wad of bubble gum. "He says, 'Walk inside the building. Look straight ahead. You turn around, you're finished.' So, like, what'm I gonna do? Like, I mean, I'm not gonna take a chance. But I'm gonna play it smart, see? Like, I'm in this building all the time. An' I know there's this security guard by the elevators. So I go in like the guy says, an' I don't turn around. An' then I run for the guard."

At this point the gum began to pop with even greater ferocity.

"An', well, like you know the rest. Jerk's not there! Whatsa point of havin' security? Right?

"Anyways. That's all I know. 'Cept fer his voice. The holdup guy. Told you that b'fore. It's, like, really deep, the voice. Like that actor. You know, whaddayacallim . . . James Earl Jones. That guy."

Jeff sighed deeply. He found he was doing a lot of that lately. Sighing. This would not have happened in Loretto, he was sure. He sighed again, wondering whether, by putting pressure on the courier, maybe arresting her, or threatening her, he could get her to tell the truth.

Jeff Ercul has determined that there is a flaw in the account the courier has given him. What is that flaw?

7

Filming at
L'Hôtel du Roi

Barney, Must — absolutely must — complete shoot before noon to be sure of the lighting. Also, rushes from Monday show that early 1940s time frame is

LOBBY SCENE: To be Reshot Wednesday A.M.
Barney King's Copy. DO NOT TOUCH!

not clear enough. Suggest you take Charlotte through the lobby much slower. Have camera linger over the three women extras in the obviously forties clothes. Maybe focus longer on their gloves and hats.

Also, I've now got a TIMES front page with a head that says "ROOSEVELT SIGNS LEND LEASE BILL". Might be overkill but we can always cut.   *S.*

VID — Establishing shot under opening credits. Medium close-up of bottom one-third or so of elevator doors. Should pick up bottom of brass scroll ornamentation. Hold two seconds after credits.

AUD — Palm Court–style music. Not loud. Lots of violin. Bring up volume when elevator doors open.

VID — At final credit, doors open to reveal two pairs of legs. Approx. knees down. One is uniform of elevator operator. Be sure shoes are lace-type. Highly polished but worn.

Barney, check this. That dumb kid wore loafers in Monday's shoot. S. ✓

The second pair of legs is elegantly feminine. Skirt just over the knees. Shoes are pumps with satin bow over toes. These legs exit the elevator. Camera follows at MCU as the legs turn and go to end of hallway. Pause at entrance to main lobby beside large candia palm. Stay on MCU while one hand comes down and checks that seams are straight. Hand has a diamond ring but not on wedding finger. Diamond bracelet on the wrist.

AUD — Low buzz of conversation noise as legs enter lobby. Does not overwhelm the music. Footstep sounds should accompany the legs.

VID — After the stocking seam check, pull back from legs for wide angle to take in whole lobby and then come back in slowly to CHARLOTTE. Make clear the legs are hers. She starts moving into the lobby. Follow her at medium long as she turns left toward the set of elevator doors on the opposite side of the lobby. CHARLOTTE slows then stops at another candia palm between her and these elevators. Camera keeps on moving to the doors, closing in but keeping full-length shot as doors open. VAN SLOTIN exits elevator. Pull back for longer shot. VAN SLOTIN walks straight toward camera. Hold camera until diamond stickpin in the tie is clearly visible. His silver-headed cane is used. Not just an ornament.

B. Get an ECU of his hair. (Guy can't act but he looks good.) Also, rushes show slight tear in left sleeve of suitjacket. S. ✓

AUD — Hold music and conversation buzz. Add more lobby-type sounds here. Bring up bell sound as bellhop crosses in front of CHARLOTTE and VAN SLOTIN with message card. Fade right out when CHARLOTTE walks into VAN SLOTIN.

VID — From behind VAN SLOTIN.

CHARLOTTE emerges from candia palms, glancing over her shoulder. This should be the first shot of CHARLOTTE from the front. Her suitjacket is buttoned. The veil on her pillbox hat covers her forehead and comes down right to the eyes. Camera stays on her for the whole of the following exchange. Both she and VAN SLOTIN are apparently distracted by the bellhop. She walks into VAN SLOTIN.

CHARLOTTE: Oh, I'm so terribly sorry! Are you all right?

VAN SLOTIN: (more than a bit confused but recovers fast) Ah . . . ah . . . why, ah, yes I believe so. Perhaps I should pay more attention to where I'm going.

CHARLOTTE: Are you sure you're all right?

VAN SLOTIN: Indeed, miss; in fact, I think I'm going to remember our meeting with some pleasure!

CHARLOTTE: Oh . . .

VID — CHARLOTTE puts out a power smile and withdraws at a speed that's just inside good manners. Camera pulls back to medium long and rolls left, following CHARLOTTE in full length as she moves toward the revolving doors at the street exit.

AUD — Music is now very faint, covered by a much more intense melange of lobby sounds. These come right up for a second or two as RAUL steps out of the alcove and blocks her path and then fade right out. No FX or music during entire exchange that follows.

VID — After RAUL blocks her path, move in to MCU for

entire exchange. Shoot speakers face on.

B. No need to reshoot the ECU of Charlotte's hand going inside Van Slotin's suitjacket. Perfect in the rushes. S. ✓

Sy,

    Agree with your comments above. Rest of scene is basically OK in the script but I want you to take the piece above back to the writers. It's the same thing that bothered me before. They've made Charlotte just too obvious a dipper. Unless they can fix it, this scene isn't going to work.

                    Barney

Why does Barney King feel that Charlotte is too obvious as a pickpocket?

8

Whether or Not
to Continue Up
the Mountain

DETAILS WERE EMINENTLY CLEAR through the lenses of the
big Zeiss field glasses. There were no fences to be seen that far
up the mountain, but then, she didn't expect any. She could
see the cattle clearly though. Could even see them placidly
chewing their cud and see their ears twitching away as they
clustered together in the weak autumn sun. Funny, she
thought. She'd never really noticed before how they seemed
to gather together like that from time to time during the day.
Almost like a planned social event. Just above the cattle,
behind a rock, a pair of ganz, timid little Alpine deer, grazed
furtively. Most importantly, she could see the path, see where
it wound cautiously around big rock formations then
zigzagged where the terrain was unobstructed but steep.
And finally, where it took a short, straight run up to and over
the top.

It wasn't the first time Chris Beadle was glad she'd just
happened to be the ranking officer present when the towns-
people pulled that SS Oberleutnant out of the cave where
he'd been hiding. That's how she got the glasses. The
Oberleutnant was carrying a Luger, too, and the famous

SS dagger, but the Zeiss was all Chris had taken. A minor bit of pilferage in light of what was going on all over Germany in the first few months following V-E Day. Besides, they had served the Allied cause well for the past year. At the moment, they were offering information that might well preclude a trek up the mountainside.

Chris lowered the binoculars to her waist and scanned the mountainside without them. With the naked eye, she noted, the path simply couldn't be seen.

"'E's not up there, m'um."

She did not turn around to acknowledge the man behind her. He was an informant whose name was Werner, or Horst, or Jeurgen — he answered to all three — who had learned English from cockney troops. Privately, Chris referred to him as "Fifty-Fifty." Four times she'd used him in her searches for accused war criminals. Twice his tips had paid off, and twice they had turned out to be not just transparent fabrications but quite possibly indications that he took money from the other side from time to time.

"'E's, not up there. Wastin' yer time, m'um."

This time Chris Beadle turned around. He stood a few steps below her, for the terrain was steep here; they'd ridden up from Feldkirk, the town beneath them in the valley, on a ski lift.

"What makes you so sure?" Chris peered directly into his eyes. That always made him look away. "Switzerland's just over the other side. Once he makes Switzerland . . ." She let the thought hang.

"Too cold, m'um. 'E'd never go up."

"Too cold? Then what are the cows doing up there?"

"Swiss Browns, m'um. Bred fer it. Likes the cold, they do. 'Im, 'e's got the asthma. Can't breathe in the cold."

Chris turned around again and raised the glasses. The Swiss Browns had begun to disperse a little. The ganz were gone. No surprise. They never stayed in one spot for more than a few minutes. It took her only a few seconds to work out the math: five tips, two good ones. That worked out to forty percent. So much for "Fifty-Fifty."

It seems Chris Beadle does not believe Werner, or Horst, or Jeurgen. What has led her to discount his advice?

9

Nothing Better than a Clear Alibi

IT WAS NOT JUST THE OLD WOMAN'S EYES that warned Nik Hall to go easy; it was the whole package. At Your Peril! was written all over her.

Beginning with her clothes. The dress, made of satin (or something equally expensive) was buttoned very carefully from bottom to top, encasing her like a fortress against all assaults. The gate was protected by a brooch that was guaranteed to be worth more than a month of Nik's salary, and matched by earrings that, well, he didn't care to speculate.

Even the physical weaknesses that should have betrayed her years — Nik figured she'd be in her late eighties at least, but he certainly wasn't prepared to ask — even these weaknesses were subdued, some by subtle means, some by force of will. An example of the former was the scarf in her lap that attempted to conceal, ever so casually, hands that were ravaged irremediably by arthritis. The latter was evident in the osteoporosis that had clearly won the battle for her spine but not her spirit, for whatever effort and discomfort it cost her, Augusta Reinhold met Nik's gaze head on. She would not be the one to blink.

It was the eyes that made Nik wish someone else had picked up the telephone an hour ago at the Major Crimes section. So dark and piercing. If the eyes really were windows to the soul, then Augusta Reinhold's had one-way glass.

She spoke first.

"Are you going to stare, detective, or do you want to hear what I have to say?"

Normally, Nik would have blushed, but somehow her question fit the pattern he'd expected. He wanted her to do the talking, and that meant she would have to lead. This was not a lady accustomed to control from outside. The only way into the fortress would be through gates she unlocked herself.

Nik licked his upper lip slowly, then the bottom one, while bringing his fingers together into a steeple. Augusta Reinhold watched him intently, the powerful eyes boring in on his face. He looked back over his left shoulder.

"In the bedroom there," he said, "was your granddaughter —"

"Who raised you?!"

Nik turned back to the eyes immediately.

"Don't you know enough to look at people when you speak to them?!"

He bowed his head in apology. The gesture let him enjoy a small grin of triumph. He'd confirmed what he suspected: that she was hard of hearing. No hearing aids, though. That would betray weakness.

"Young man." Augusta grabbed the reins with authority. "Let us get on with this. What you need to know is that my granddaughter was with me when that fool was shot. I won't pretend I'm unhappy he's dead, the parasite, but it was not Siobhan who did the shooting. She is impetuous, I'll grant you. How else could one account for her marrying him so hastily? Marrying him at all! And he abused her terribly. You'll have no difficulty verifying that. But she was out in the hall with me when the shots were fired."

Nik sat expressionless. He already knew that three bullets

had brought about the untimely end of Paisley Wendt, and that the noise of three shots had issued from Suite 5 within a minute before or after 11 A.M. Confirmation of the time had come from two different tenants and the building janitor.

"I was in my solarium having coffee with Esther. That's Esther Goldblum. She's in Suite 14 right across the hall from me. My only neighbor, and a widow like me. We have coffee together every morning when we're in town. Until quarter to eleven. That's when Esther leaves to do her trading. Currencies, mostly. Don't like them. Never have. Too much depends on strange little people thousands of miles away.

"No matter. When Esther left, I went and got dressed as you see me now. On Thursdays I have lunch at the League, you see, and I always take Siobhan. You can verify that easily, too.

"When I got off the elevator here on the third floor, Siobhan was waiting to get on. She was coming to get me, you see. And before you ask, there was no one else on the elevator. It was right then we heard the shots in her suite, and well, the rest is . . . is distasteful, to say the least."

"Mrs. Reinhold." Nik was careful to look straight at her this time. "Do you have a companion or a maid or housekeeper?"

A flicker of wariness crossed the dark eyes.

"Raythena comes in every day at one. She stays as long as is necessary and does what is necessary."

"And how many shots did you say you heard, Mrs. Reinhold?"

The flicker grew to a smolder.

"I didn't say."

"Yes, indeed. Excuse me." Nik spoke very softly. "Er, how many shots do you recall hearing?"

"You think I'm deaf, don't you?" The eyes were sparking now. "That's why you're almost whispering! Well, I'll tell you how many shots I heard. No! First, I'll tell you what you just said. You asked me how many shots I recall hearing, didn't you! I heard three, young man. Three!"

Nik bit down on his lower lip. He took a chance and looked back over his left shoulder again. What he had to decide, and fast, was whether to press harder on Augusta Reinhold to ferret out the truth, or instead to push on the granddaughter. In the end, it was the eyes that helped him decide to go after the younger one. Even if Siobhan was as tough as her grandmother, she had to have softer eyes.

What has led Nik Hall to believe that he is not getting the truth from Augusta Reinhold?

10

Guenther Hesch Didn't Call In!

SUSAN VINT STOPPED WITH ONE FOOT in the doorway of the little room, then leaned back and motioned to her partner to come take a look.

"Just what you'd expect," Bill Willson said, more to himself than for anyone else's benefit. "Probably hasn't been a surveillance base this neat on the entire planet. Ever."

Susan grinned and stepped into the room with Bill right behind. The two were careful about where they put their feet but it didn't take much effort. Instead of the usual flotsam that covered every available space in a room being used for a stakeout, this place looked more like someone had been preparing for surgery. A telescope stood poised and ready between a shuttered window and an adjustable stool, and except for a small table in one corner and an old-fashioned chrome and ersatz ivory ashtray stand beside the telescope, there was no other furniture.

There were no fast-food wrappers either, and no pizza boxes, no newspapers, and no electronic games — nothing to betray the tedium that accompanies surveillance.

On the table sat a camera with a telephoto lens, a cellular

telephone, and a small bowl made of orange glass.

"Bet you the filters are in there," Susan said, and took a few steps to the table. She looked in the bowl and smiled grimly, first to herself, then at Bill Willson.

Bill nodded. "Nobody more predictable than Guenther Hesch." He took out his pen. "Go ahead and count 'em. Then we can tell how long — God, it stinks in here! I can't believe the way he smokes! He even rolls some of them. Every four butts he cranks into a roll-your-own. Him! For a neat freak, it doesn't add up."

Bill Willson and Susan Vint were in command of a four-site surveillance. Guenther Hesch, assigned to one of the four sites for the 8 A.M. to 4 P.M. shift, had failed to make the check-in call at 1:15 P.M. Normally a single missed call would not have triggered a quick visit like this from the two chief operatives, but this was Guenther, and Guenther was the most obsessive-compulsive person they knew.

Guenther Hesch wore a brown serge suit on Mondays and Wednesdays, a tan check on Tuesdays and Thursdays, and the jacket from one with the pants from the other on Fridays. He had three ties and wore them in rotation on consecutive days. He went to a movie matinee every Saturday afternoon, and every Sunday ate breakfast at 8:15 in a highway diner that served the same special week in, week out. Guenther always arrived at his assigned work sites at exactly three minutes before the beginning of a shift, and no one had ever known him to be late, even when impossible weather snarled traffic to a standstill. Even his dreaded chainsmoking habit was compulsively regularized. He never smoked in his car or in his apartment, and not at headquarters. He only smoked on surveillance, lighting a cigarette on the hour, and precisely every fifteen minutes thereafter.

Guenther was fanatically intolerant of any disruption of his routines and would go to any lengths to ensure this would not happen. Unfortunately he was so annoying to his colleagues that Bill and Susan constantly scrambled to find assignments like this one where he could work alone. One former partner, while pleading for reassignment, had described Guenther as so uptight that he could sit on a lump of coal and create a diamond in four days. Another had come screaming into headquarters because he couldn't stand to watch Guenther's habit of snapping the filter off cigarettes and smoking them from the freshly defiltered end. A third had resigned rather than face a second pairing with him.

Still, in the words of the commissioner, Guenther Hesch was a "keeper." He was never late, never sick, and never asked for favors. Needless to say, he not only made every required check-in call while on surveillance duty, he made them to the scheduled second, and when the 1:15 P.M. call was not forthcoming, it took no time at all for Susan and Bill to agree they needed to see for themselves.

"Seventeen," Susan said. "And a butt. Something's wrong."

"I agree," Bill replied. He frowned at Susan Vint. "No sign of a struggle, no note anywhere. Phone works. I don't get it. He was here. Why didn't he call?"

How do Bill Willson and Susan Vint know that Guenther Hesch was still in the surveillance site at 1:15 P.M.?

11

Right Over the Edge
of Old Baldy

DIRECTLY AHEAD ABOUT TEN PACES OR SO, a double white blaze on the trunk of a large oak told Pam Hall the trail turned sharply to the right. She paused for a moment, putting out her hand to lean on another oak. The edge of Old Baldy was just ahead but Pam chose to stop anyway to enjoy the moment. It was her favorite time of year, every hiker's favorite: early fall.

Absently shifting her backpack to a more comfortable spot, she let her eyes drift across the multihued canopy above her. Then she looked back down the trail toward Kimberley Rock, where she'd stopped for a drink of water about ten minutes ago. From Kimberley on there was almost no underbrush on the Bruce Trail. Just huge, old-growth forest enclosing a deep silence that even the birds respected, a silence that went right into the soul. It was like being in an empty cathedral in the late afternoon, one of those moments that all hikers know they share with cloistered monks and nuns.

Perhaps it was the silence. Certainly it was the deep peacefulness, the precious sense of the moment, that made the scream leave such a ragged tear in Pam's consciousness. It began as a moan. Even though it lasted only a second or two, this was the part that would linger more intensely than any other in her nightmares. At first it sounded almost like pleasure, not unlike the aaahs one frequently heard from people who first encountered the vista from the lip of Old Baldy. But there was no pleasure in this moan. It turned from an "aaah" into an "iieee" and then into a long "nooo" that faded out and away like oil running down a funnel. Someone had gone over the cliff.

Later, when Pam was explaining her suspicions about Hadley Withrop to the officer from the Park Service, she realized that the entire event had taken place only a minute or so ahead of her on the trail. It had been two years since she'd hiked this part of the escarpment and she wasn't aware she was quite so close to Old Baldy when it happened. That became another part of her nightmare. Had she not stopped at the double blaze to drink in the quiet, would Sheena Withrop still be alive? Or would she, Pam, have been pushed over the edge too?

Either way, she'd gotten there too late. When the scream first pierced Pam's senses and the logic of what was happening finally tumbled through, she found herself gripping the oak tree in panic with both hands, wasting precious seconds in the process of absorbing the shock. In her nightmare the next sequence always came back in slow motion: the bending over to pick up her walking stick and then inadvertently kicking it away so she had to bend again; the slosh of her water bottle working its way loose in her backpack as she ran up the trail, affecting her balance; the spiderweb that grabbed the bridge of her nose and pushed into both eyes as though it was trying to capture and hold her right there in the middle of the trail; the sight of a pair of turkey vultures circling high out over Beaver Valley, oblivious to the drama below them; and then, as she came up to the shaking Hadley Withrop at the edge of the cliff, the echo of Sheena's cry. An "aaah" and an "iieee" and a "nooo" all over again, in precisely that order.

She was sure she had heard an echo too. Positive. And her nightmare confirmed it. But it was also the part of her account that made the officer from the Park Service exchange quick glances with his partner. The doubt in their faces was plain.

"As I came up to Baldy," Pam told the officer, "he — Withrop — is standing there. Well, not quite standing. He's kinda bouncing around. You know, upset. Pacing.

"I think I really scared him. He obviously wasn't expecting anyone. Certainly didn't know I was on the trail. But he didn't say anything about that. He just said, 'She went over, she went over.' But not panicky, you know, not all cranked up like you'd expect. He talked to me like we'd just met on the trail. Casually, you know, as people do.

"'We just came up from Kimberley,' he said to me. 'Ate our lunch at the rock there. And we weren't here two minutes when . . .' Now that's when he started to cry. Went down to his knees and put his face in his hands, and started to shake. Really sounds like shock, doesn't it?

"But here's why I don't like his story, Officer," Pam added emphatically. "And I don't think you should like it either."

What is Pam Hall about to tell the officer from the Park Service that will explain why she doesn't accept Hadley Withrop's account of what happened?

12

Sunstroke, and Who Knows What Else!

LYING PRONE ON HIS BACK with his wrists tied to stakes, Evan Strachan was keenly aware of his vulnerability, so he spoke to his sister with the least possible assertiveness. She was two years older than he, as well, something he could never get himself to discount.

"I still don't see why you can't get Pindaric to do this," he said. "It's his case."

Sara wouldn't have noticed his tone anyway. She was too preoccupied with a pair of stakes and with pieces of nylon rope that she had wound around her brother's ankles.

"Because you're about the right size," she replied. "Pindaric, on the other hand, is a fat slob. And a jerk," she added. "He's profane, obscene, and vulgar. He hates women. And he's got dog breath. Need more?"

"Guess that about covers it," Evan mumbled.

"Besides," — Sara's explanation wasn't finished — "he's head of the firm. And the head of the firm doesn't lie on his back on a rifle range and let a law student tie him to stakes!"

"Not at the glorious firm of Brutus, Judas, Machiavelli and Quisling anyway!" This time Evan's tone suggested more

43

confidence in his opinion. "Lawyers!" He blew at a long blade of coarse grass that kept tickling his face in the early morning breeze.

"I told you to stop calling it that! It's Pindaric, Pindaric, Krafcywcz and Steinberg. They're creeps but they're going to hire me when I graduate. Now move up a bit so I can put these ankle stakes in the exact same holes too!"

"But then the sun'll be in my eyes," Evan protested. "This way I get some shadow from the stake. It's hot already, in case you didn't notice, and it's gonna be a scorcher. Or do you want me to get sunstroke too, like that kid?"

For the first time in several minutes, Sara Strachan drew her attention away from tying down her brother's ankles, to look back at the first stage of her handiwork. Evan's wrists were tied to stakes, angled into the ground. He was lying in precisely the spot where, forty-eight hours before, Cadet J. D. Elayna had submitted himself to the indignity that had allegedly put him into intensive care at Etobicoke General. According to reports, his chances of complete recovery were still slim at best.

Cadet Elayna had run seriously afoul of the rules at Nobleton Military Institute, and under the self-discipline policy followed by the school, his barrack-mates had decided to stake him to the ground below a target on the rifle range, where he lay during a morning practice with live ammunition. He'd survived that part (physically at least), but then he'd been left there on a day that turned out to be the peak of a week-long heat wave. By the time the school's administration found out and intervened, the cadet was dehydrated and totally delirious. Whatever emotional trauma he had suffered was still undetermined, but his parents hadn't waited to find out. They'd already formally notified the Nobleton Military Institute of their intent to sue, and the Institute had immediately retained Pindaric.

Sara's eyes narrowed. She was deep in thought and didn't notice that her brother was scratching his still untied ankles by crossing one over the other and drawing them back and forth like a carpenter with a handsaw. She was only vaguely aware that he was talking to her.

"Do you know how to tell if lawyers are lying, Sara?" he was saying.

"Evan," Sara said very softly.

"Their lips move."

"Evan," she repeated.

"How can you tell the difference between a dead skunk and a dead lawyer on a highway?"

"Evan!" Sara got to her feet. "That cadet. He could have got up and walked away if he wanted to! Well, not when the bullets were flying, of course, but right after!"

How has Sara Strachan come to this conclusion?

13

Should the Third Secretary Sign?

HAD SHE BEEN MORE OF A FEMINIST, Ena Mellor would
likely have raised Cain, or at least been resentful, over the fact
that last spring's round of promotions had gone exclusively to
men. But she wasn't particularly intense about her feminism;
nor was she the type to hold a grudge. Besides, she'd gotten a
bit of a prize in any case. Her rank may have continued to be
Third Secretary, which she'd been for the past two years, but
now she was Third Secretary at the embassy in Vienna instead
of in Cairo.

For Ena the transfer meant an apartment in which the
plumbing worked as a rule and not an exception. There was
no baksheesh to pay every time she needed anything done.
She could picnic in the grounds of the Schonbrunn Palace
with no beggars playing on her guilt. There were concerts —
oh, were there concerts! Mozart, Beethoven, Mahler . . . And
museums. And churches. And history. Ena knew that if she
had pushed hard last spring, she might have become a Second
Secretary, but in Katmandu. Hard to get good schnitzel in
Katmandu. No, Third Secretary in Vienna was definitely a
better deal.

Admittedly, the Soviets had messed up her pleasure temporarily. When their tanks rolled into Prague last month and forced Alexander Dubcek and the Czech government to accept "normalization," a flood of refugees had spilled into Austria. Most of them ended up in the Traiskirchen camp. Among other things, the location of the camp interrupted Ena's now thoroughly established habit of lunching at one of the street cafes in St. Stephen's Square. Still, Traiskirchen wasn't all that bad, for it was set in a vineyard near the city.

What bothered Ena a lot more was making decisions that deeply affected the lives of the refugees. Her signature at the bottom of a single document could mean freedom for a refugee. Without her signature, the applicant could well be sent back to the repression behind the Iron Curtain. It was a power that made Ena Mellor extremely uncomfortable.

Well over half the refugees had no papers, for they'd fled that night of August 21 with only the clothes on their backs. Ena often had to rule on the truth of an applicant's identity on the basis of a driver's license, or a photograph, or a work card. Yesterday, the only proof one refugee could offer was the few koruny in her purse.

The man who sat before her now offered her a first, however. He had no passport — nothing unusual about that for someone from behind the Iron Curtain — no driver's license, no work card, in fact, nothing but a very worn and creased photograph. Nevertheless, it was a photograph that certainly suggested his life would be in danger if he were returned to Czechoslovakia, and police officials there knew he was coming.

The picture had been taken in Moscow. Even without Ena's experience in foreign affairs, she would have recognized Red Square and the Lenin Mausoleum. It took a magnifying glass, however, to see that the man in front of the Mausoleum was also the man sitting nervously on the other side of her desk. The same glass showed, very clearly, that he was vandalizing one of the USSR's most important monuments by painting over Lenin's name. Most noticeable was that the

"L" had been changed to a box, and the "I" had been altered to resemble a Byzantine cross. How he had accomplished this in the middle of Red Square, with all the guards about, was incomprehensible to Ena, but it was a crime that, if he'd been caught, would have meant a long stretch in a gulag. Still, how he'd done it was not Ena's problem. Her problem was whether or not to sign his application.

Should Ena Mellor sign the application? Why, or why not?

14

A Successful Bust
at 51 Rosehill

WHEN WORD GOT AROUND THE SQUAD that geraniums had figured in the high-profile drug bust Jack Atkin made at 51 Rosehill, no one was the least bit surprised. As the rumor went, Jack had bolted upright out of a sound sleep at 4 A.M., shouted "Geraniums!" into the darkness, and within less than two hours there were narcs all over the illicit lab on Rosehill.

Jack's partner explained it all to the others in the squad that afternoon, down in the coffee room. She and Jack had entered 51 Rosehill late the previous day — with a warrant, of course — and found absolutely nothing. At least, nothing illegal.

That was contrary to expectations. The stakeouts were convinced that the townhouse at that address held a tiny but very efficient lab where cocaine was being diluted and bagged for street sale. Yet, as Mandy Leamington had said, "When me 'n' Jack did the search, there wasn't a thing that'd say drugs.

"It's like somebody made them with a cookie cutter, those townhouses," Mandy had explained. "They all look exactly the same. Same size, same shape, same everything top to bottom. And they're all the same size and shape inside too. Like somebody made a bunch of boxes and set them one on top a' the other. Thirty a' them. Fifteen each side a' the street. Woodington Manor, it's called.

"Anyway, you go in from the back, from the parking area. Like, the back door is really the front door. Weird, eh? OK, so you step in, and you're on a landing that's halfway between the basement and the first floor, and there's a staircase on the left, six steps down, and beside it, one that goes six steps up. To the first floor. We went down first, and on the wall across, facing west, there's this shelf under the window well, with a two-seater sofa under that, same length as the window. And there's geraniums on the shelf. Five of them. Really gorgeous. Big blooms and red as can be.

"'Course, you know Jack. Place could be on fire but he's got to check the geraniums first. You know how he always sticks his middle finger into the pots?

"Me, I head right for one of these massage chairs they got in there. You know, the big easy chairs that vibrate? They got rollers to go up and down your back? Really pricy. Coupla grand, right? And they got two a' them! Jammed in on each side 'tween the sofa and the wall. So I sit in one a' them, but it's not plugged in. Jack, he sits in the other, when he finally gets his finger outa the geraniums, that is. Now, that one works, we find out eventually, but he doesn't find the switch at first 'cause there's no lamps and it's kinda dark, and we didn't turn the overhead light on 'cause, well, you 'member that Lake Rosseau bust when the light switch was booby-trapped?

"Now here's the real deal. Upstairs on the first floor, they got two more a' these chairs! Can ya believe it? Set up just like the basement! Sofa in the center, below the window, just the same. Shelf full a' geraniums. Gorgeous geraniums again. And these chairs on either side! Only thing different is these got nice lamps beside 'em this time, on end tables. Oh yeah, and six geraniums instead a' five. Jack says there's more light so they can put more on the shelf. Squeeze 'em together a bit. Lotsa books upstairs too. We figured this is where they do their reading 'cause there's no TV up here. But these chairs!

Y'ever sat in one a' them? We gotta get one in here. Yuh can be asleep in five seconds!

"Anyway, I says to Jack they may not be into drugs but into stolen massage chairs, but he doesn't even hear me. Got his finger in the geraniums again, and lookin' out the window, checkin' the sunset and mumblin'.

"Got to hand it to him, though. It was him that figured out they were hidin' a lab."

How has Jack Atkin figured out that a lab has been hidden?

15

The Case of the Body
in Cubicle 12

"SUICIDE, BUT I DON'T BUY IT."

Aaron Penfold spoke without looking at his partner, who was also named Aaron — Aaron Walmsley. Back on the third floor at District 18 headquarters they were known as A-1 (Penfold) and A-2 (Walmsley) or, more frequently, as "Double-A."

A-2 was standing just inside a main entrance door, in an office cubicle. It was one of thirty such cubicles, each precisely the same size and configuration, all squeezed into a large, windowless, rectangular room. Each cubicle had half-walls with tiny quasi-doorways opening into a quasi-hallway that ran around the inside circumference. The only departure from this cookie-cutter design was a raised dais in the center of the room. Five steps led up to a platform where a circular desk with a hole in the center commanded an aerial view. A chair stood inside the doughnut-shaped desk. The supervisor's chair.

"Yeah, but . . ." A-2 had arrived some time after his partner and was still getting a feel for the scene. "Sure seems like the kind of place that would drive someone to suicide."

He took a single step, managing to cross the hallway by doing so, and stood at the entrance to Work Area 12. From there, he could see the note in the printer.

"Sorry," it said. "But there's just no point."

It wasn't signed.

"What do they do in here, anyway?" A-2 continued. "Place looks like a bunch of fattening pens."

A-1 pulled his gaze away from the body of a woman slumped over the counter in the cubicle. At first glance she was of indeterminate age, but the neatly coiffed hair covering the upturned side of her face appeared to be naturally black, suggesting she was likely younger than older. She sat in a standard-issue, armless office chair, with castors designed to roll her efficiently across the Plexiglas platform that covered the standard-issue gray broadloom. Her torso lay across a desk blotter that took up the only flat space on the counter.

As for the rest of Work Area 12, it was obvious that computer equipment had priority. There was a gooseneck lamp with a strangely incongruous Tiffany-style shade, but it had to fight for its spot behind a hard drive. Beside one of three keyboards sat an inkwell and an ornate fountain pen that, whatever the woman's age, was certainly older than she had been. Everything else was plastic and high-tech metal alloy — hard drives, a scanner, three screens, three keyboards, and a printer. Work Area 12, like the rest of Work Areas 1 to 30, was geared to output.

"They're programmers," A-1 replied finally. "The sweatshop of the twenty-first century. They spend their miserable working lives in these boxes, grinding out software for their masters until the next technical revolution, and then they're tossed because they're as outdated as the equipment they work with. Friend of mine — he's a real techie — says these people last about five years."

Aaron Walmsley grimaced and stepped forward to look more closely at the bottle that lay open beside the woman's right hand. He used a tweezers to lift it so that he could read the pharmacist's label and verify his prediction that it had contained barbiturates.

"One on the floor too." A-1 pointed at another prescription bottle under the counter. It too was empty, and had rolled under a Gordian knot of wires and connectors and surge protectors to stop against a pair of patent leather, high-heeled pumps.

"Downers?" A-2 asked.

"Uh-huh. More of the same. If both bottles were full, she got at least eighty pills down. Enough to do the job."

"Yeah, but I agree. I don't think it's a suicide either."

Why are both Aarons convinced that the situation they are investigating is not a suicide?

16

The Case of the
Broken Lawnmower

NEITHER WOMAN WORE A UNIFORM, so that standing on
the sidewalk that paralleled the quiet street, both looked more
like suburban housewives having a morning chat than detectives (first grade) from Homicide Division. Mary Blair stood
with one hand in her pocket, the other on her hip. She was
frowning at a small rectangle that Kristy Bailey had just spray-
painted onto the lawn that edged the sidewalk. For her own
part, Kristy was looking with some distaste at the yellow paint
that, despite great care, she'd managed to get on her fingers.

They were the first ever mother-daughter team on the force
and for that reason attracted a degree of media attention
which made the commissioner extremely uneasy. Fortunately
for his peace of mind, the commissioner had no idea that dialogue like the following was a regular occurrence between
these two high-profile officers.

MARY BLAIR: (*wrinkling her nose at the painted rectangle*) The
only spot on his front lawn where you can see between the
houses across the street there, into the alley.

KRISTY BAILEY: (*rubbing thumb and forefinger*) Darn stuff is so sticky.

MARY BLAIR: Everywhere else the view is blocked by something. Houses, trees, the victim's garage with that purple door. Guy probably deserves to die for painting it that color.

KRISTY BAILEY: Took almost a week to get it off last time.

MARY BLAIR: (*stepping into the rectangle*) And it's precisely this spot where his lawnmower handle comes apart.

KRISTY BAILEY: Makes my fingers look like I smoke roll-your-owns! Such an ugly yellow!

MARY BLAIR: So our witness turns off the mower and then hears a shot. Looks up to see his neighbor getting it in the chest. Very coincidental!

KRISTY BAILEY: Yeah, but this is where we found the nut.

MARY BLAIR: The what?

KRISTY BAILEY: The nut. It came off the bolt right here, and then the lawnmower handle came apart. You know, for want of a nail the shoe was lost, for want of a shoe . . . Like that.

MARY BLAIR: I've got yellow paint on my toe!

KRISTY BAILEY: (*taking Mary's elbow*) And there's the bolt! Over there, about five or six steps away. Almost on the sidewalk. I wonder how we missed it earlier?

MARY BLAIR: Should be able to get it off with kerosene, don't you think, or cleaning fluid?

KRISTY BAILEY: Just goes to prove again, you can't check too many times.

MARY BLAIR: We got kerosene back at the station?

KRISTY BAILEY: Janitor probably does.

MARY BLAIR: Right! Never thought of that! Wonder why the witness lied.

KRISTY BAILEY: Well, that's our next step, isn't it?

MARY BLAIR: Let's go back right now. We've got to do the paper on this anyway. (*Steps very carefully out of the rectangle.*) Imagine! Painting your garage door purple!

KRISTY BAILEY: Actually, it's puce.

MARY BLAIR: That's even worse.

Why do Mary Blair and Kristy Bailey conclude that the man mowing the law was lying?

17

A Quiet Night
with Danielle Steel?

"Could be we've caught a bit of a break, Steve. According to the list of emergency telephone numbers at the kitchen phone, her regular physician lives two doors east of here. That'd be the odd-looking house with the cupola over the front portico? No lawn? Pushed right out to the street almost? There's a patrolman on the way over there right now. Maybe we can wrap this up without needing to do an autopsy. Almost for sure, no inquest, right?"

To anyone unacquainted with Steve Lanark, it would have looked like he was paying no attention whatever to his partner. Chantal Breton was used to these stone-faced responses, though. They had worked together for several years in a one-two ranking in the coroner's office. In fact it was widely expected that Chantal would take over as chief when Steve retired in three months, and widely held that she deserved to do so.

Chantal kept talking. "What we've got isn't all that dramatic, except maybe for the Jacuzzi." She wrinkled her nose and stared with dispassionate professional interest at the body lying in the now-cold water of the large bathtub.

"Woman in her late forties. Executive. Married and divorced twice. Lives alone. Sunday night she pours a scotch, fills the Jacuzzi, picks up the paperback she's got going, and gets into the tub. There's no marks or bruises, no signs of violence, no bumps on her head or back of her neck. She's even wearing her glasses.

"Tell you what." Chantal Breton looked around to be sure none of the police officers in the next room could hear. "I'll give you two to one the physician tells us she had a bad heart. Or very high BP.

"No, I'll go you one better! I'll give you *three* to one that if we have to do an autopsy, we don't find water in the lungs. Like, she died before going under the water. OK?"

Steve Lanark still behaved as if he did not even hear his partner. Instead he was hunched over a small ersatz marble slab on one side of the bathtub. It was about the size of an end table and, indeed, was designed to serve that purpose. At one corner of the slab, farthest from the tap end of the tub, a facecloth in a deep burgundy lay folded neatly with a bar of soap sitting on top. Neither had been used. At the diagonal corner, within easier reach, was a cocktail glass, its bottom still covered with the remains of a drink. Scotch, the two doctors had concluded earlier.

Steve appeared to be using the platform as a mirror to examine a shaving cut on his chin. The marble was ivory, with subtle streaks of gray and an occasional hint of ocher. Its surface was pristine, like the rest of the place, and gleamed in the high light.

"Really neat, this woman, wasn't she?" Chief Coroner Lanark spoke for the first time. He lifted his face from the side platform, but still didn't look at Chantal. "I mean, look at her robe there on the floor. She folded it before getting into the tub. How many people do you know do that?"

He got to his feet, arched his back, and then tapped first one foot on the floor then the other. "New shoes," he said. "I hate new shoes." He twisted his right foot like someone extinguishing a cigarette butt. "This whole place . . . Why don't you give one of those cops out front there a three to one that they can't find a toothpaste spatter on that mirror there above the sink?"

"Or a dust bunny under her bed?" Chantal added. "Yeah, she's neat all right. Or else her cleaning lady comes in every day. I know what you mean about the shoes, by the way. You should try it from my end. Men have no idea at all what shoe designers do to women's feet. I mean, they expect that —"

"Help me lift the book out of the water." Steve interrupted what he knew would otherwise become an extended commentary on women's podiatric tribulations. "I think if we use that long-handled shoehorn over there, we won't have to get ourselves wet."

Silently Chantal went over to the back of the bathroom door and lifted the necessary implement off a hook and brought it over to the tub. It slid easily under the sodden paperback.

"Danielle Steel." Steve made no effort to control the distaste in his voice when he saw the cover. "Now tell me, is a woman like this going to read this kind of stuff? I mean, she's CEO of her firm, a big success. Appears to be a totally nonsense type. I mean, Danielle Steel?"

Chantal sighed with the patience of one long inured to male obtuseness. "Hey, it's her own private bathroom. It's the end of the day. She's got a Jacuzzi. She's having a drink. You want her to read Kierkegaard or something? Give me a break!"

Steve pursed his lips and nodded. "Yeah, I guess not," he agreed finally with a sigh, although his tone suggested he was not entirely convinced. Then he added somewhat grumpily, "And before you offer, I'm not taking any bets on whether we find more novels like this in the rest of the house. Whoever was in here after this woman died wouldn't be that stupid."

On what basis does Chief Coroner Steve Lanark conclude that someone was in the bathroom after the victim died?

18

Vandalism at the Bel Monte Gallery

ROBBIE DEXEL PACED BACK AND FORTH on the sidewalk, forcing himself to go slowly and deliberately, at a measured pace, but his distress was obvious. Every few seconds he would stop, put his hand to his mouth, and cough hard. Then the pacing would resume. Alongside him, in the street, cars passed by in a regular rhythm. On the other side, just a few feet away, under a chestnut tree that towered over the building behind her, a uniformed police officer watched with interest. Eventually she grinned and spoke.

"Stomping back and forth like that isn't going to get them here any faster, you know. I mean, they're late. The roads are icy. Nothing we haven't encountered before."

Robbie stopped and glared hard at her. "Hey, it makes me feel better, OK? You got a problem with that? I prefer to walk and cough instead of stand and cough. Now if that bothers you then, then . . . Look, I'm sorry. It's this lousy cold. Makes me so cranky. Happens this time of year without fail. Ever since I can remember, just before before Christmas I get a cold."

Officer Dale Dunn grinned again and nodded. She moved a few steps closer.

"No problem. I'm not much good at waiting either, really. And I don't have a cold! Quite frankly, I don't see why we can't wait inside in the gallery instead of out here in the cold."

She waved at the building behind her. It was a two-story, turn-of-the-century brick structure, very tastefully renovated. The whole street was like that: restored buildings that housed boutiques, all of them upscale shops with limited hours and one-of-a-kind inventory. The facing immediately behind Dale framed a large wooden door, which in turn held a brass plaque announcing in delicate letters that the Bel Monte Gallery awaited its very special clientele on the other side.

"At least if we were inside," Dale went on, "we could look at the paintings. A lot more interesting than staring at the traffic out here."

Robbie took a deep breath, slowly, so that he wouldn't make himself cough. He spoke slowly too, trying to get a whole sentence out without having to clear his throat.

"We have to wait out here," he said, "because here is where the new witness says he was standing when he saw the job being done."

Robbie was referring to an incident at the Bel Monte Gallery that had taken place several months previously. During the night, someone had broken into the gallery through the roof, thereby defeating the security system, and had damaged a number of very valuable oil paintings by slashing them with a knife. The police had made an arrest within days, however, and at that very moment in the county jail one of the city's best known art collectors, Marc-Jean DiBeau, was being held without bail for his upcoming trial.

Dale had been the arresting officer and Robbie was the investigator from the agency that had insured the paintings. The two of them had returned to the Bel Monte site together because of a somewhat startling development. A witness had surfaced the day before, telling a story that put an entirely new twist on the case. It was their job now to question him, and they wanted to do it at the scene.

Dale pointed up the street to where a police patrol car had pulled over to the curb. "Here we are," she said. "Our witness." She lifted her eyebrows at Robbie. "Don't be shocked."

Robbie pivoted slowly and focused on the two people getting out of the car. One was a police officer, an older man, the other, well, in spite of Dale's warning, Robbie couldn't quite restrain himself.

"Him? That's the witness? He's a streetperson, a . . . a bum!"

Dale shrugged her shoulders. "Think about it. Who else is going to be out here at two o'clock in the morning? This is a commercial district. There's nobody living here. By the way, his name is Patchy Lomax."

"Patchy?"

"Look at the clothes. What would you call him?"

As Patchy and his escort came closer, Robbie swore he was looking at a circus clown. There was barely a spot on Patchy's clothes that was not covered by squares and rectangles of every imaginable texture and hue. Perched on top of this kaleidoscope was a mass of crinkly gray hair that grew up and down and out, covering every facial feature except for a very red, round nose that moved like some kind of battery-powered toy.

Patchy wasted no time. "Up there. Up there at the window, 'at's where I seen her." A skinny, nicotine-stained finger appeared out of a rainbow sleeve and pointed at a window on the second floor of the Bel Monte Gallery. "'At's where I seen her do it. Slash them pictures. Big woman. Tall. Lotsa hair. Long. An' I seen her. No question."

Robbie frowned. One of the partners who owned the gallery was a tall woman with long hair. He started to talk but the coughing took over, so Dale asked the obvious questions.

"OK, so you saw a woman at the window, but you're going to have to do a lot better than that. What were you doing here at two o'clock in the morning? And it's dark then. You can see in the dark maybe?"

Patchy raised his red nose in the air. Another skinny, yellow-brown finger appeared, this time pointed accusingly at Dale. Before Patchy could speak, Robbie interjected.

"What we want to know more than anything is why you didn't tell us all this four months ago when it happened. Why now?"

The finger was joined by its colleagues, the grimy hand now held out like a traffic cop, first at Robbie, then at Dale. Patchy lifted his red nose even further. With great dignity, he turned to the bus shelter a few feet from where they were standing. "In here, lady cop." He took a step and turned to Robbie. "You too. It's answers you want? Then one at a time. We start in here."

Both Robbie and Dale followed obediently; neither of them caught the smile on the face of the older officer.

"I was in here," Patchy announced once he was fully satisfied he had everyone in place and fully attentive. "'Cause you could tell it was gonna rain hard."

Robbie stole a quick glance at Dale. Patchy was right about that. It had rained the night of the break-in, a harsh downpour that, according to the weather office, had begun at 2:15 A.M. and lasted about ten minutes.

"Now yuz look up there." The finger came out again, leading them back to the second floor. "That winda'. Right b'tween them branches there. Ya see? 'At's where I seen 'er, 'cause the lights is on all the time in that buildin'. Leastways all night they are. Ya knew that too, didn't ya, lady cop? Tryin' t' fool old Patchy, weren't ya?"

Through the labyrinth of hair, Robbie could see a pair of dark eyes gleaming triumphantly. He took a long breath very slowly and said, "But this doesn't explain why you waited all this time to tell anybody what you saw."

The gleaming eyes bored into the young investigator's. "Well, young fella, it just happens that I don't read the art news every day. How'm I supposed to know that somebody has ruined a painting? So far's I know, she mighta been doin' that 'cause she was supposed to. Ya know, cuttin' it up and then callin' it art.

"Anyways, I didn't know nothin' about this until I met yer Mark John Dee Bo fella down at th'county. Some right interestin' people in that jail from time t' time. Anyways, ya got the wrong guy. It was a woman done it. I seen her."

Without waiting for a response, Patchy Lomax turned and left the shelter, heading back to the police car that had brought him. Dale Dunn, meanwhile, continued to stare at the window, as did Robbie Dexel, each waiting for the other to speak.

It was Robbie who finally broke the silence. "Pretty solid, you agree?"

Dale nodded.

"I almost bought it," Robbie continued. "You too?"

Dale nodded again.

Apparently, neither Robbie Dexel nor Dale Dunn have been convinced by Patchy Lomax's story. Why not? What's wrong with Patchy's version?

19

Laying Charges
Too Quickly?

HOPE ROGERS STARED ABSENTLY at the empty chair opposite her, letting the back of her mind speculate on the truth of the old adage that bad things come in threes. If it was true, she felt, then she and her team were due for a turn of luck. Three times in the past several months, the empty chair had been filled for meetings like this by DeWitt Thompson-Cruze, the most inept — in Hope's opinion — prosecuting attorney she'd ever had the misfortune to deal with since she'd become Senior Investigator. Three times Thompson-Cruze had bungled the cases she and her colleagues had so carefully worked out together. This afternoon's meeting would launch their fourth together. If the wheel of fortune had any grease on its axle, as Hope fervently prayed for, her success rate just had to roll into better times.

"Should I start anyway?" Don Reilly's voice startled Hope. Don was the team's case analyst. "I've got that presentation at four, you know. To the Safety Commission?"

Hope replied without releasing her gaze at the empty chair. "Give it another minute. The traffic out there doesn't make distinctions between lawyers and idiots, so maybe he —"

A loud crash in the hall and a sudden opening of the door announced the arrival of DeWitt Thompson-Cruze.

"Elevator," he said, making circular gestures with his left hand, more or less in the direction of the hallway. No one was sure what he meant, but no one really wanted to know either.

Don Reilly cleared his throat and, when he had Hope's attention, asked "Now?" with his eyebrows. Hope held up her hand just slightly.

"DeWitt, are you quite ready now?" she asked.

"Elevator was jammed," he replied. "Couldn't reach the button for the seventh and I had to ride up to ten, and then it expressed . . ."

"DeWitt!" Wayne Brogan spoke for the first time. He made everybody jump. "DeWitt, shut up. Okay? This is about the Scalabianca murder. The rest of us want to get on with it. Now if you feel you can concentrate . . ."

Hope indulged herself in the putdown for just a few seconds, and then quickly turned the team to business.

"Go ahead, Don," she directed.

"The videotapes are being sequenced and numbered as we sit here," Don began. "Should be ready later this afternoon. Maybe we . . ." He paused to let Hope fill in.

"We can see them individually," Hope said. "I want everyone to do that, by the way. But tomorrow afternoon, same time, we view together. Everybody clear on that?" She looked pointedly at DeWitt Thompson-Cruze. "At 2 P.M.?"

There were nods all round.

"Just give us the summary for now," Hope said to Don, who immediately began reading from his notes.

"Loredana Angelica Scalabianca. Aged fifty-four. Wife of Nunzio Gregorio Scalabianca for thirty-six years. 241 Lambeth Gardens, that's over in the Albion Park district. Found yesterday morning by her daughter, at . . . at . . ." He shuffled his notes several times. "Eleven, no — ah, here it is! At somewhere between ten to and ten after eleven. Daughter's not absolutely sure."

"We're onto that, Hope," Andy Biemiller broke in. "The daughter's, uh, name's Theresa Manno. She's pretty sure now it was before eleven. I'm seeing her later today. She's kind of shook up, needless to say."

Don waited for Andy to add more. When it didn't happen he went back to his notes. "M.E. puts time of death at about 4 A.M. yesterday morning. Body was found in the kitchen. Severe blow to the back of the head, but her head, neck, and shoulders were wet. Water on the floor too." Don looked up from his notes. "What it looks like, I mean, you can judge for yourself from the videotape, what it looks like is that she was surprised. Well, I don't know about surprised. Anyway, it appears the murderer came at her from behind, bonked her and either she fell into the sink or he held her in to finish the job. You know, drown her?"

"Why 'he'?" Wayne Brogan wanted to know.

Hope looked over her glasses at Don, who replied without animosity. One of the purposes of these meetings was to challenge assumptions.

"Granted," Don replied with a nod. "But the victim was a big woman. At the very least, the perp would have to be good and strong."

"The daughter's no will-o-the-wisp, for what it's worth," Andy chimed in. "She's got to go 145 pounds or more. And that's power big, too. She's not fat."

"OK," Don conceded. "He or she — the perp — it seems, hit the Scalabianca woman and then — this is appearances again — drowned her."

Wayne Brogan held up one hand. "Before we go down that road any farther. My examination shows she was killed by the blow. No water in the lungs, not even in the mouth or trachea."

Hope pressed a little. "But her hair and neck and shoulders were wet?"

"Well, not soaking," Don clarified. "I guess, more on the damp side, but definitely not from perspiration. Somehow her head and shoulders were in water."

"What on earth was she doing at the sink at four o'clock in the morning?" Hope asked.

"I've got that," Andy said. "You want it now?"

"You got any more?" Hope asked of Don.

"Just the videotape," Don replied. "You said you only wanted summaries for this meeting."

Hope nodded. "OK, Andy, let's have yours."

Andy didn't use notes. "Nunzio Scalabianca, the husband." He cleared his throat and began again. "Nunzio Scalabianca does ornamental metalwork. Apparently he's really an old-world-type craftsman. An artist. One of the uniforms at the scene is into that stuff. Said Nunzio is the one they all want to be like. Anyway, he's freelance. Works in a shop out the back. His story is that because of the heat wave, he'd reversed his schedule. Was working nights."

Andy shifted in his chair and looked briefly at DeWitt Thompson-Cruze, who'd been writing busily. "That's credible, I'd say. He's got all that hot welding equipment. There's a forge in the shop too. Anyway, he says that Angie — he calls her Angie — has been having real problems sleeping for the past year. According to him, her behavior's been totally weird for a couple of years now, and getting worse. Gets up and goes to the kitchen at all hours. The daughter verifies that. Stubborn woman too, according to the daughter. Wouldn't wear her hearing aid any more, for example."

"The way I have it," Hope broke in, "Nunzio was supposedly off at a job site a mile or two away. Is that right?" She looked at Andy for confirmation.

Andy nodded.

"So his hours are just as offbeat as hers," Hope added.

Andy nodded again. "No witness for this," he said. "No night security at the job site. I've got some uniforms canvassing the neighbors right now. Maybe one of them went to the can at 4 A.M. and happened to look out.

"Anyway." He shifted in his chair. "Here's the damning

69

piece. We found a ball peen hammer at the bottom of the toolbox he carries in his car. Cheap thing you can get at any department store. Stood out 'cause it's new. No marks on the head or dirt on the handle."

"Prints?" Hope asked.

Andy shook his head. "Wiped. But not carefully enough. We got some blood off it. Ninety-five percent certainty it's hers. We'll get to 99.9 with DNA. That's by tomorrow, I hope."

Wayne broke in. "Ball peen hammer's consistent with the cause of death. Three blows. Likely died immediately from the first one. Dead center in the back of the head."

"Right- or left-handed?" Hope asked.

"Right," Wayne answered and then looked at Andy. "Nunzio right-handed?" he asked.

DeWitt Thompson-Cruze waited for Andy to nod "yes" and then jumped in. "Sounds like enough to me," he said to Hope. "I'd say we stop wasting time and charge this Nunzio."

Each of the others watched Hope carefully. Hope had trouble suppressing a grin.

"DeWitt," Hope spoke slowly. She was looking out the window. "You ever heard of the old saying that bad things come in threes?"

Thompson-Cruze shook his head, frowning. He had no idea where Hope was going with this.

"What I want to know is, when there's a fourth," she continued, "is it really the fourth, or is it in fact the first in a brand-new series of three?"

Thompson-Cruze's frown deepened, but Hope didn't wait to let him articulate his confusion. "Because if you've missed the obvious hole here," she said pointedly, "Nunzio's counsel is going to bury you in it."

Hope Rogers is aware of a weakness in the case that, in her opinion, would preclude laying any charges against Nunzio at this stage. What is it?

20

Taking Down the Yellow Tape

SERGEANT SAGER'S VOICE CARRIED right through into the washroom, adding to Geoff Dilley's agony. He was sure it was Fate, some powerful, enduring curse that had been visited on a misbehaving ancestor and had now passed down to him. There was certainly no other reason, at least not a logical one, to explain why, of the six sergeants in 42 Division, he had to land in Sager's section. She was career-driven, demanding, unreasonable, and impossible to please. In Geoffrey's opinion anyway. Sager was even to blame for the stomach cramps that had driven him to the washroom for over half his shift. Had he gone to his regular Friday poker game the night before, as both his instinct and his inclination told him to do, instead of to Menna Corracci's retirement party just to please Sager, then he wouldn't have eaten egg salad sandwiches. It had to be Fate, for he never missed poker. And worse, he never ate egg salad sandwiches. It was the egg salad — he knew this for sure — that gave him the cramps that had kept him in the station for his entire shift, instead of out in a patrol car where he much preferred to be.

"Constable Dilley!" For the second time Sergeant Sager's

voice pierced through three sets of concrete block walls. Geoffrey hunched down in the cubicle and braced himself for another wave of cramps.

"I say! Constable Dilley!"

Why couldn't the woman say "Geoff" or "Dilley" like every other section leader in 42 Division? And the accent. Did she always have to sound like a docent at the Tate Gallery?

"He's in the washroom, Sergeant Sager." This time Geoff heard Frank Paul's voice. Frank had shared the reception desk over the shift. Did most of the work too, Geoff had to admit. He'd lost track of how many times he'd run to the washroom over the past eight hours.

"Well, tell him to attend at my desk before he leaves."

Geoffrey gritted his teeth and fought off another impending cramp as he exited the cubicle. He had to get out there and "attend at Sager's desk." He owed it to Frank.

"You wanted me, Sergeant Sager?" It occurred to Geoff as he walked in that he might not have buttoned his uniform properly; her fixation on proper attire was legendary. But if that was the case, she didn't notice.

"The Lindenmacher site, Constable Dilley. It's on your way home, isn't it?"

It wasn't a question. The site of this recent murder was a good twenty minutes out of his way and Sager knew it, but Geoff made no reply.

"I've just been notified by 'D' Court that the suspect has been denied bail, and charges will be laid tomorrow morning." Camilla Sager, thus far, had not taken her eyes from the papers on her desk. She was making small tick marks in the margin of a document. "Now, the site. I cleared it yesterday. Signed it off personally. But just in case, I left the yellow tape in place." For the first time she looked up at Geoffrey. "One is wise to be patient in situations like these."

Geoffrey neither spoke nor nodded. He knew that annoyed her.

"Since it's on your way, would you mind awfully . . ."
— she leaned hard on the "awfully" — "going round and
removing the tape. The real-estate people have been allowed
in to begin cleaning up. I gave them permission. But I don't
want those people taking the tape down. Even touching it."
She made "those people" sound like bacteria.

Geoffrey held off responding as long as he could without
being blatantly insolent, and then nodded. The truth was, he
didn't really mind. Especially if the cramps left him alone.
The Lindenmacher murder was 42 Division's first big case in
a long time and offered more excitement than most of his
colleagues were used to.

Dietrich Lindenmacher lived alone in a country home,
where his mutilated body had been found by the rural mail
deliveryman. It appeared he'd been killed in his own bed, first
struck on the head and then had his throat cut. A suspect was
arrested in less than six hours and right now was two floors
below in 42 Division's holding cells. He'd been there a week.
The local media had buzzed with praise of the division's
quick work in apprehending the murderer.

As Geoff approached the site a few minutes later, glad to be
finally out of the station, he could see that the real-estate
people had come and gone already. Their For Sale sign leaned
against the open gate, ready to be tamped into the ground as
soon as the yellow tape came down. They'd been cleaning
too, just as Camilla Sager said. The raccoons had already been
at the garbage bags set out at the road for pickup. He stepped
carefully through a litter of empty soup and dog-food cans,
and kicked aside a completely shredded box that, despite the
damage, still proclaimed its point of origin as Deedee's
Doughnuts.

"This would have to have been last night. Or near dawn
today," he said aloud, musing on the thoroughness of the
raccoons. In a sardonic way, it pleased him that they hadn't
waited for permission from Sergeant Sager.

He walked on, curious. Although Geoff had not been on

the investigating team, he, like everyone else in the division, was familiar with the details. Robbery appeared to have been the motive. Lindenmacher's VCR was missing, as was the TV, as well as several small appliances. Lindenmacher must have had a laptop too; Sager had found a manual for one. Interestingly, not one of the items missing from the house had turned up anywhere. Not in the suspect's van, and not in the hands of any of the known fences in the area.

The suspect had vigorously denied everything about the case. He was a vagrant, with no fixed address except for his van, which apparently had been his home for some time. The van had been seen by three different witnesses on Lindenmacher's side road on the day before his body was found, and given that the road was one that went from nowhere to nowhere, there was really no good reason for a stranger to be on it. The kicker, however, was that the suspect had a record. He was on probation for two B&Es.

Geoffrey peered through the picture window at the front of the house, into Lindenmacher's sitting room. Ordinary enough, but the big easy chair had a great view of the valley across the road. Moving to his left toward a second window, Geoff's foot caught on a small coil of electric wire. A small piece of yellow tape hung from it and fluttered in the breeze. This must be where the guy jumped the burglar alarm circuit, he thought. That conjecture was confirmed when he saw the cut wires under the sill of the second window. He shook his head. Pretty clever, he thought. But maybe not quite clever enough.

The wind was coming up a bit stronger as Geoff Dilley walked back to his car. He still hadn't taken down the yellow tape, and he wasn't going to. It suddenly occurred to him that he hadn't had a single stomach cramp since turning into Lindenmacher's driveway.

"Could it be?" He was musing aloud again. "Could it be my stomach is feeling better because Sergeant Sager has quite possibly missed something?"

As he opened the car door he concluded with more than a little pleasure that this was likely the case.

What clue, or clues, has Geoffrey noticed that Sergeant Sager apparently may have missed?

21

Problem-Solving in Accident Reconstruction 101

BY THE END OF THEIR SECOND DAY at the police academy, students taking Accident Reconstruction 101 from Chief Instructor Barry Stranks invariably learned that once he settled back in a chair and lit his pipe, they had been given all the information they were going to get in order to solve an assigned problem. That's why the class had immediately dispersed into two almost equal groups as soon as Lieutenant Stranks sat down. One group had wandered down the hill, checking both sides of the road for evidence. They were now measuring the distances between the shoulders of Humber Trail Road and the respective edges of the large, swampy pond that the road bisected. Most of them were already slapping at mosquitoes.

The members of the other group were only a few steps away from their teacher, studying the chalk marks on the road.

"Your first driver," Barry Stranks had told them, "the one approaching from the west, her story is she was simply coming down the road, minding her own business, when the other driver, the one coming up from the east, swerves to miss a big turtle and crosses the yellow line. So the driver from the east is now in the wrong lane. The first driver responds by swerving to the south side, but her right front wheel gets pulled down in the soft shoulder."

He had paused then and looked at them all. "Everybody with me so far?

"Now, you're going to have to use your imagination here," he continued, "as well as your logic. Obviously this accident is hypothetical. We can't afford to be wrecking cars every time I teach this course. However, I've chalked the spot on the road right there, where she says the turtle was. In fact, two of you are standing on it!"

Immediately two of the students shifted over, with sheepish grins on their faces.

Chief Instructor Stranks continued. "Just down there a bit, on the other side, I've also marked the spot where she hit the shoulder."

He paused to be sure everyone was listening for the next piece of information. By this time he had taken out his pipe and held it, unlit.

"Now here's the rest of the scenario. This driver tries to pull back onto the road but overcompensates and crosses to the north side, onto the shoulder further down there." He pointed with his pipe. "I've chalked it; you can see. But now the angle of entry is too obtuse and she goes right off the road and into the swamp. Car's a write-off."

He took out a lighter and held it over his pipe. "Any questions?"

"The other driver, sir?" one student ventured hesitantly.

"Indeed." Barry Stranks put the lighter back in his pocket. "The other driver carried on. Took off. Unless you can find a witness — and in a case like this you should assume you're not going to; country road, midsummer afternoon, light traffic, no houses nearby — all you have is the account by the driver going west."

The students parted as Barry made his way toward the lawn chair he'd unfolded a few minutes before. "The issue is insurance," he said as he sat down, taking out his lighter again. "It's a matter of assessing fault. If our eastbound driver was making legitimate and sensible avoidance moves because somebody pulled into her lane, then there's no fault on her part. On the other hand, without a witness . . ." He held up both hands and shrugged. "Could it be she wants a new car and set this whole thing up?

"What you have to do is reconstruct this event as best you can and then analyze it. Is it a straight story, or is there a hole in it?"

With a motion born of long practice, Barry put the lighter to the pipe and settled deeper into the chair.

"Most of the time," he said between puffs, "a class can solve this in one pipeload."

In the accident scenario Chief Instructor Stranks has constructed, is the driver's account plausible, or is there a "hole" in it?

22

Before the First Commercial Break

DIRECTOR'S NOTE: Edit this piece to three minutes ten seconds.

Insert between credit and first commercial break.

SCENE ONE

Camera Notes for Storyboard, Scene One:

#1. Pull back so that entire prison building can be seen. Gilhooley appears from behind wall in distance and walks into camera toward gate. Hold until Gilhooley reaches gate.

#2. Track him to motorcycle west of gate where rider is already astride. Move in as Gilhooley boards motorcycle behind rider. Hold close for a view of back and side of rider. Pick up rider's leather vest, cutoff T-shirt, long hair, and snake tattoo down length of left arm.

#3. Track left to follow motorcycle as it drives away and out of shot.

#4. Fade to black.

FX, Scene One:
Sound of Gilhooley's footsteps builds as he walks toward camera. Voiceover of Assistant Warden Brackish starts after footsteps are established. Sound of idling motorcycle comes in over Brackish's last words. Motorcycle sound follows Gilhooley and rider out of scene and fades.

Script, Scene One:
ASSISTANT WARDEN LEONARD BRACKISH: (in voiceover) Getting to be a habit, Mr. Gilhooley, isn't it? What's this, our third goodbye? No. Let's call it an au revoir. Men like you, Gilhooley . . . it's not a case of if but when. You'll be back, and I'll be waiting. You're bad, Gilhooley. Just bad seed. Like a snake. You can't help yourself. You're poison.

SCENE TWO

Camera Notes for Storyboard, Scene Two:
#1. Establishing shot of seedy storefront from across street.

#2. Move in and pan slowly left to right over gold lettering on door: RARE COINS AND ESTATE JEWELRY

#3. Continue panning right, pulling back until shot encompasses Gilhooley talking to another man on sidewalk. Arms are moving to emphasize what he is saying. Man has snake tattoo on arm. Might be biker from Scene One but dressed better. Listens and nods. No face.

#4. Continue pan past two men and fade to black.

FX, Scene Two:
City traffic noises.

No Voices in Scene Two

SCENE THREE

Camera Notes for Storyboard, Scene Three:

#1. Inside store at rear. Full shot. Gilhooley stands on one side of rear door and police officer on other side. Gilhooley wears slacks and shirt with long sleeves rolled to just above wrist. He is cowering. Officer is in uniform. Her stance is confrontational. One hand on door handle as though to keep Gilhooley from running. On the floor between them is a revolver. Back of butt is against the door so that muzzle points at camera. To her left and in front, Katzmann sits in a wooden chair.

#2. When Katzmann begins talking, move back to pick up array of shelves above him and scatter of diamond and ruby rings on working surface behind him. Katzmann wears loupe like a monocle, raised to his forehead. All his dialogue is emphasized by a rigidly pointed index finger at Gilhooley, the officer, and the door.

#3. Gilhooley gives impression he'd like to be sucked into the wall. Throughout scene fingers the barrel of the middle hinge on the door. While talking, retreats back along the wall a few inches but continues to hold the hinge as if for security. With right hand gropes behind him feeling for a small table just inches away, but never makes contact until the final shot.

#4. Gilhooley's hand bumps the small table, nearly upsetting a cup of coffee in a Styrofoam cup. He turns to rescue it and for a split second reveals a snake tattoo on his arm.

#5. Fade to black.

No FX in Scene Three

Script, Scene Three:
KATZMANN: . . . and two minutes after I see Gilhooley talking to this guy — another bum — the guy's in here with his gun out. He's been tipped off, no question. 'Cause he comes right to the back here. This is where all the good stuff is, the really valuable pieces. I mean, how does the guy know to do that unless he's been told? Right, Gilhooley?

GILHOOLEY: I didn't say nothin' t' him 'bout that.

KATZMANN: And there's no way the guy's going to know I've got the safe open this morning to work on the new stuff unless he's been told. And, AND, who leaves the security screen wide open? The one separating this area from the rest of my store? You see what I get, officer, for hiring parolees? If it wasn't for my alarm system . . . I dunno. As it was, I thought he was going to shoot me anyway. When the alarm went off, I mean. But he panicked. Dropped his gun and run out the back door. That's when his partner here came back.

GILHOOLEY: Look, it just ain't like that! He — like, Katzmann — sends me across the street for coffee. That's every morning this time. The guy on the street? I never seen him before. He was just askin' directions. Alls I know is I come back here with the coffee and the alarm's ringin' and then you cops come in. I don't know nothin' what he's talkin' about!

If it is the director's intent to have viewers wonder whether Gilhooley is guilty or is being set up, then the director is going to have to correct a serious mistake before these scenes are shot. What is that mistake?

23

More than One
St. Plouffe?

"THIS IS LUDICROUS. You've got a written confession, written and *signed* confession, but you've also got two different suspects claiming it's theirs?"

"Yup."

"Two different suspects with exactly the same name?"

"Unnh."

"Alfred-Louis St. Plouffe — *Junior?*"

"Yup."

"And they are father and son?"

"'S right. Father and son."

Struan Ritchie looked up from the confession. "Careful, Kamsack, you almost spoke a whole sentence!"

Effam Kamsack raised both eyebrows in the general direction of his boss and took a deep breath. "Yup," he said again.

Struan waited a second or two just in case there might be more, but he knew from experience that it was more expedient just to forge ahead.

"Now, just to add to the astounding clarity we are all enjoying in this case, it seems there are actually *three* living Alfred-Louis St. Plouffes," he continued. "Senior, the original; then his son, Junior, and then Junior's son, Alfred-Louis St. Plouffe the Third?"

Kamsack leaned forward again and with his right index finger tapped the report lying in front of Struan. "Yup," he said for the fourth time, and then folded back into a slouch.

"Except that the Third has always called himself Junior also, so in effect there are two Juniors?"

"Unnh."

"So the confession I'm reading here, signed Alfred-Louis St. Plouffe Junior, is claimed by both the Juniors?"

The toothpick in Kamsack's mouth elevated ever so slightly. Struan took that as a "yup." The fifth.

"Well, thank you, Detective Kamsack," he said. "I couldn't have laid it out more clearly myself!"

Kamsack took a while before responding with a grunt, but Struan by then had turned to the source of their mutual interest. The confession was typed on plain white bond paper and signed in a clear, unelaborate script, one that would be simple to forge. The information itself was but three short paragraphs.

On 1 May last, I administered poison in the form of arsenate of lead, to Her Ladyship Teresa Elana Giurgiu, formerly the Countess Covasna of Romania.

Her Ladyship attended mass at St. Sofia's on 1 May, as has been her uninterrupted custom on each of Romania's national holidays since the abdication of King Michael in 1947. During her absence, I added the aforementioned substance to the medicine she consumed three times a day. The effects of the substance, along with all other pertinent details relating to her demise, are known to the police, and I do not dispute their findings or conclusions.

I hereby stipulate that what I have written here is offered of my own free will and without coercion.

Alfred-Louis St. Plouffe Jr.

"You know, Kamsack," Struan began, but then stopped abruptly. Kamsack was shifting the toothpick from one side to the other, a sure sign that he was about to volunteer something.

"Got 'em both here for yuh," the detective said very softly. "Think you'll wanna talk to 'em. One a' them's spinnin' yuh 'bout the confession." He slowly undulated to his feet. "Here." He tossed a sheet of paper on Struan's desk. "Ask 'em both these three questions."

Before Struan could react to the longest discourse from Kamsack he could recall in some time, he found himself facing the elder St. Plouffe Junior and, after a few preliminary probes of his own to which the suspect was entirely forthcoming, asked the first of Kamsack's three questions.

"What intrigues us, Monsieur St. Plouffe, is your motive. According to our findings, Lady Giurgiu had very little money . . ."

Alfred-Louis cleared his throat. "Your findings are correct. She had very little money. Indeed, she was nearly destitute, excepting for some ornate jewelry, which I'm convinced she purloined from the royal treasury in 1947."

Struan nodded, using the movement to glance surreptitiously at the second question. "But then, why?" he asked. "She was just a harmless old lady."

"Not harmless when she was younger. Previous to King Michael's abdication, she fabricated a web of intrigue that effectively dissolved our family's fortune. In fact, my family as well. It killed my mother. I can give you the details if —"

"Not just yet," Struan interrupted. "Before we go any further, I have to ask if you are fully aware of the possible consequences of your confession? We have the death penalty in this jurisdiction, you know."

"Yes, I know. But I am not adverse to the idea of death. Not now that I have satisfied the family's honor. And incidentally," — St. Plouffe moved to the edge of his chair — "I'm also fully aware that you have to decide between my son and myself as to who is guilty. He foolishly advanced the premise to one of your investigators that it was he who poisoned the Countess. A noble act, but one you should ignore. I did it. The confession is mine."

Struan avoided eye contact with Kamsack while ushering the elder St. Plouffe Junior out of his office and the younger one in. The father and son were remarkably similar in appearance and behavior. In manner of speech too, for to the first of Kamsack's three questions, the one about Lady Giurgiu's financial state, the younger St. Plouffe replied, "Indeed. Unless I have been misled — a distinct possibility, by the way; she was remarkably devious — the Countess Covasna was, how shall I put it, er, impecunious."

"But then, Monsieur St. Plouffe, it's only natural that I ask you *why*." By now Struan had allowed himself to become fascinated with the whole process. "What did you have to gain from poisoning an old lady?"

St. Plouffe's lips curled but didn't quite lift into a smile. "Because of that *old lady's* activities when I was a young child. My health —" He stopped abruptly. "Look, this is superfluous to the matter at hand. I poisoned her. And I am fully cognizant of the potential consequences. Those are the only points about which you need concern yourself. As to my father's attempt to divert you from the truth by claiming authorship of my confession, I can only say that while his gesture is a noble one, it is futile."

Struan stole a quick glance at Kamsack, who was basking in a huge grin. The grin continued long after both St. Plouffes were deposited in the outer office. And it stretched to the limit when Struan said, "My hat's off to you, Effam. Pretty clever. We've got a lot more digging to do on this thing, that's for sure. But at least we know who wrote the confession."

Which Alfred-Louis St. Plouffe has written the confession?

24

When the Oxygen
Ran Out

THE ROOM WAS SPARSELY FURNISHED and, as a result, uninviting. There was only one place to sit: a single, straight-backed chair, a refugee from an uncomfortable dining room suite, that sat disapprovingly in one corner, just to the left of the window. Under the window itself, an old-fashioned hot-water radiator hissed softly. More or less in the center stood a burnished walnut end table. It was highly polished but had no gleam, and it didn't match the chair. Behind the little table, there was a floor lamp with a shade that may once have been ivory-colored but had aged now to a russet orange. Altogether, though, there was enough furniture for the room. More would have made the place seem crowded. With or without the dead man in the wheelchair.

As it was, the dark wooden bookshelves, and the deep brownish-red rug, and the heavy, flocked wallpaper made the room appear even smaller than it was. The first thing she would do if it were her place, Fran Singleton decided, would be to lighten it up. Get rid of the wallpaper first. Maybe even paint the shelves, although that would take some courage, for they were genuine oak. Solid too, no veneer. And the rug.

To her, the color choice, especially in a room like this, was almost a criminal act.

Fran always redecorated her surroundings when she found herself in an unpleasant situation. It took her mind off grim details that she didn't want to deal with. In this case, it was the not-unexpected demise of the late Humbert Latham.

She was not here by choice.

"All you've got to do is sign the death certificate," Lenny Stracwyz had pleaded over the telephone. Lenny was the county coroner and a classmate of Fran's from med school. He was in the Bahamas on vacation and had asked Fran to do him this favor, for he had no intention of leaving the beach to return to the cold of Toronto in January.

"Just sign the death certificate for me," he had repeated when Fran hesitated. "There's no question he's dead, from what I gather. Natural causes. Simple as can be. It just needs a signature. You don't have to do anything else — except, uh, uh, well, maybe you'd better make a few notes just in case I have to call an inquest."

Fran had tried to say something at that point but Lenny Stracwyz cut her off.

"Just sign," he said. "Please? Make it official? So I don't have to come home? You don't even have to do time of death; that's done already. OK?"

The mention of a possible inquest had made Fran more hesitant than ever, but the plaintiveness of Lenny's voice had pushed away her natural reluctance. She had wanted to remind him that she was a pediatrician and didn't "do death," but in spite of that she found herself, less than an hour later, holding the cold wrist of Humbert Latham, confirming the nonexistent pulse.

The body of the old man still sat, bent slightly forward, in the wheelchair where he had died. His silver hair, always so perfectly groomed, reflected the lamp's wan glow, lending an impressive dignity to his death pose. Except for the slightly odd position, and the bit of drool that had dried along his chin and on the lapel of his blazer, Humbert Latham looked much as he must have when he'd been wheeled into the room yesterday afternoon, but somehow, more peaceful. There was less pain in his face than Fran remembered from the last time she had seen him. That was after the stroke. And the hands with their clawlike gnarl — she particularly remembered the hands because her own patient, Latham's great-grandson, was terrified of them — their once frightening, crippled grip seemed to be quite relaxed now. In a sense, Humbert Latham almost looked relieved that the oxygen had run out and he could finally let go.

Fran checked the oxygen bottle under the seat of the wheelchair and then followed all the tubes and checked each connection. They were all properly in place and intact.

"Sergeant Hong from homicide says it ran out between three and four this morning and the forensic specialist says he stopped breathing about fifteen minutes after that." It was the voluble rookie cop assigned to guard the scene. Sergeant Hong had not spent much time in the room. He'd simply ordered that everything remain untouched and had headed off to headquarters to coordinate the search for Latham's night nurse.

"Too bad, really. The poor old guy." The young policeman was still talking. "Lousy way to go even if it looks like he wasn't going to be around much longer anyway. I mean, you're totally helpless and you depend on someone to change your oxygen, and she doesn't show up. I mean, Jeez. Then the day nurse — I mean, like, she's the one who started all this — she's the one that finds him dead this morning!"

Fran knew the details and tried to ignore the prattle.

The day nurse regularly wheeled Humbert Latham into this room in the late afternoon so that he could enjoy the winter sunset through the west-facing window. At least everyone speculated that he enjoyed the sunset. The stroke had taken away Latham's ability to communicate. The nurse had left him alone there as she did every day at this time, and then had left the house five minutes early. Latham's valet, a man with a reputation for ironfisted control, had given her permission to do so, and had also arranged for the night nurse to come in early. It was the night nurse's job to take the old man down the hall to his bedroom, connect a fresh bottle of oxygen, and prepare him for sleep. But the night nurse had never shown up, and as yet had not been located.

"And that valet, Mr. Latham's 'gentleman'?" The policeman was leaning closer to Fran now, trying without realizing it to capture her full attention by hovering over her. "I mean, he's always here, right? Anyway he's supposed to be. But what does he do? He has a car accident! With that big Rolls. Just goes to show you, a patch of ice don't respect the make of your car. Anyway, so he gets taken to the hospital, all woozy and can't talk. So poor old Mr. Latham's got nobody. No nurse, no valet . . ."

Fran turned and leaned into the young policeman's face. He had been saying "val-ette," and that bothered her almost as much as his interference.

"It's 'val-AY.' Like the letter 'A.' French. And I know all this."

She turned to the window and took a breath, surprised by her vehemence. The morning sun was now reflecting off the windows on the building across the street, and the beauty and promise of it calmed her. Slowly, and just slightly self-conscious, she turned back to the officer.

"There's a security guard on the grounds at night, isn't there?" The more the thought took hold of her the more she forgot her annoyance. "There is if I remember correctly. Seems to me he gave me a hard time once when I came on a house call."

The policeman looked at her uncomprehendingly.

"Because," she went on, excited now, "unless he too was missing last night — seems like everybody else was — I'd bet

Sergeant Hong will want to know if he's the same one that's on every night."

Why is Fran Singleton interested in this information about the security guard?

25

The Terrorist
in Fountain Square

SPECIAL AGENT CONNIE MOUNT took a sheet of cleansing tissue out of her shirt pocket and carefully wiped the eyepiece of the telescope. There was no need. The lens was spotless. But she cleaned it anyway, without paying the least attention to the task. It was a way of keeping her hands busy until she had to make the final decision.

Connie looked at her watch: 8:57. Three minutes left before she had to send in the team. Three minutes in which to be sure she was making the right choice.

One more time, she bent to the eyepiece and sharpened the focus on Fountain Square. The big instrument didn't need focusing any more than the lenses needed cleaning, but she was working on automatic. The only information her mind would process now was what she saw before her in the square.

A few years ago the telescope would have picked up spruce branches and not much more. This had been a spruce forest then, a piece of open country in its third life. The first had been its natural state, also a forest, mostly spruce, ironically enough, all of which the settlers had cleared. The work, though, had been in vain, for they had only managed to turn it into a wasteland. Reforestation then brought the spruce back, but this third phase lasted only twenty years. The spruce were taken off again to prepare for stage four, its present one: a shopping center, a structure so ultra-modern that, except for a few embarrassed birch trees clinging to life in big concrete pots, there was no wood to be seen at all. Just shiny aluminum, red brick, and clear glass, shaped into stores that surrounded a square made of still more aluminum and brick and glass.

At the center of the square sat the elaborate fountains that gave the place its name. With the precision that only a computerized drive system could muster, these fountains came to life every four minutes, and for exactly thirty-seven seconds, twelve jets of water shot toward the roof, while on the surface of the pool, large, viscous drops looped in mesmerizing, continuous arcs around the edge. It was this simple but attractive feature that, far more than the fountain jets, brought the patrons to stare.

Connie was watching five of them right now. Actually, four patrons and a terrorist. One of the five people staring at the water loops was carrying a switch for a bomb. The bomb was already in place, somewhere in the shopping center. That much she knew. She also knew, or at least was convinced, that the bomb was not yet armed. Someone was going to remedy that deficiency with a switch, and Connie's task was to put her team on that person — by 9 A.M.

She looked at her watch again. Just two minutes now. If only there were a bigger team, or time to bring in more people. Then she'd simply scoop up all five. That was one way to be sure. But there wasn't a bigger team and there wasn't more time. She had three agents concealed in three different stores around the fountain. Connie herself would be a fourth, but participating in the scoop would blow her cover. Even then, the best she could hope for would be to get four of the five people in the square. No, a mass grab was no good. The team had to get the right person, and there would be only one chance to do it. In two minutes — less than that now — the stores would open and people would start filling Fountain Square. All five down there could scatter in seconds if they chose to.

Connie resisted the urge to adjust the eyepiece yet again as she concentrated on the man dressed in blue overalls and yellow hard hat. He was wearing yellow work gloves. On the back of his blue shirt, yellow letters declared him to be an employee of "Your Friendly Telephone Company." Connie called this one Number Three. He had come into the square ten minutes ago, carrying a coil of rope over his left shoulder. He'd walked directly to a big steel grate in the floor, just a step or two from the edge of the pool, and he'd been standing there ever since.

Number Four in Connie's inventory was a painter. He'd only come in a few minutes ago in his white cap, white T-shirt, and paint-spattered white overalls. Number Four had come in with a paint tray and roller under one arm. In the other hand he carried a can of paint which he'd pried open and was now stirring as he sat on the floor, leaning against the wall of the pool. Four was the only one not looking at the water.

More than once in the past few minutes, Connie had felt a surge of admiration for the manufacturers of her telescope. With only a small twist of the knob, she'd been able to zoom in on the painter's hands to see that the paint under his fingernails was real. The same twist had shown calluses on the palms of Number Two, the street cleaner.

Number Two had appeared at almost the same time Connie had set up her equipment fifteen minutes ago. He carried a canvas bag over his shoulder, and in his hands a short broom and hinged shovel. There had been only a few pieces of litter to gather up, and now, like Number Three and Number Four, he had parked himself by the fountain.

In front of the Wells Fargo office, farther from the fountain than the others but staring at the looping water drops, was

Number One. She was a short, painfully thin woman dressed in a severe gray business suit. On the pavement beside her, the polished finish on her briefcase reflected the halogen lighting panels that beamed from the top of each storefront. Connie had checked the briefcase carefully. It was not new, just well cared for.

Unlike Number One, who had been as still as a mannequin the entire time, Number Five, the last one to enter the square, was steadily on the move. And no wonder. She was a professional dog walker, or certainly seemed to be. Three dogs were leashed on her left hand, a pair of overweight cocker spaniels and a somewhat perplexed shelty. Two entirely unruly Afghans pulled constantly at her right hand. In the past minute or two, the walker had settled into a pattern which took her and the dogs around the perimeter of the square in a counterclockwise fashion.

For the last time, Special Agent Connie Mount looked at her watch. "Fifteen seconds," she muttered to herself. "This better be right." She turned to the tiny microphone pinned to her lapel. "Twenty-one, do you read?"

Immediately a double click sounded in her receiver.

"Twenty-two?"

The same pair of clicks followed.

"Twenty-three?"

This time there was a gap of a second or two but then the clicks came through.

"OK. I'm giving the count. Break out on five. Here's the one you go for . . ."

Which of the five people in the square has Connie selected as the most likely terrorist?

26

A Matter
of Balance

NOT UNTIL THE FOLLOWING MORNING, a Monday, did
Tom Jones conclude, yet again, that life is a series of balanc-
ings. Maybe not quite Newtonian, he felt, in that every reaction is equal and opposite to the initiating action; more in the
sense that the events of life roll back and forth over a fulcrum
of fate, so that things even out inexorably over time.

This notion had been exemplified twice the evening
before, the first time in the elevator of the Federal Building
on Danforth Avenue. Tom had been first to board the elevator and, as was his wont, he'd stepped politely to the back.
Although only two more people got on, Tom got the unmis-
takable impression that one of them, the marine lieutenant,
had deliberately and rudely jammed him against the back
wall, keeping him there until the operator let the officer off at
the fourteenth floor. Lording it, Tom understood. Big people
often did that, especially the younger ones. But what the
marine obviously didn't know was that what he confidently
believed to be his commanding, uniformed presence was
undermined by dandruff. A bad case too, trailing so far down
his back that Tom held his breath each time the sway of the

elevator rocked him closer to the man's protruding shoulder blade.

Balance, Tom realized. Nature equaling things out. It was almost pleasant, if just a touch malicious, to contemplate the officer's embarrassment when he discovered that his image of himself had been betrayed.

A second reinforcement of Tom's reflections on balance he owed to a radio program that night. Well, perhaps not entirely; his own listening skills deserved some of the credit too. When the FBI had telephoned him just after dinner, Tom had been preparing for a quiet evening, looking forward to an unhurried scan of the as yet unread sections of the Sunday paper, interrupted by a few chuckles from the *Chase and Sanborn Hour* on NBC at eight o'clock. Tom Jones, like most of the country, was a devoted follower of Edgar Bergen and Charlie McCarthy and rarely failed to have his radio on, on a Sunday night.

But then the call had come.

"Just a few moments of your time, ah, tonight, Doctor Jones," Agent Bronowski had purred into the telephone. "A matter of national security. The Bureau is appealing to your sense of duty. That's why the timing is, well, rather unusual, I admit. However, I'm sure you'll understand the importance when I explain."

It had taken almost an hour to get to the Federal Building, and when he entered through the revolving doors, Tom had realized, for perhaps the very first time, that not everyone listened to Edgar Bergen on Sunday nights. The doorman, obviously not functioning in the role his uniform dictated, was standing under the wall directory, totally absorbed by his radio, tuned (rather loudly) to a CBS station, which was pouring forth a paroxysm of anxiety about some alien-looking cylinder that had landed in New Jersey and had just incinerated some state troopers who tried to approach it.

Tom waited for the elevator just long enough to hear a station break remind listeners that they were listening to a drama. The doorman didn't hear that, however; he'd been racing for the bank of telephones at the other end of the lobby. Many others didn't hear it either, apparently. The next day the morning news described a major panic in the streets that night as a result of the radio show.

Once again, Tom realized, balance had asserted itself. He had been dragged out of his home on a Sunday evening and into what could have been very serious danger. On Danforth Avenue alone there had been several dozen injuries. Yet he'd missed the entire imbroglio, sitting in the FBI's fifteenth-floor office.

The meeting itself lasted far longer than Agent Bronowski had promised, almost the first hour alone taken up with the agent's sycophancy.

("We realize, Doctor Jones, what an imposition this is on your time. After all, Sunday evenings are precious to us all, heh, heh, heh. But I'm sure you understand why we have to be circumspect, heh, heh, heh.")

("For someone of your stature, Doctor Jones, it must be an unaccustomed phenomenon for you to be asked to attend elsewhere. Surely you are more accustomed to be the summoner than the summonee, but then you see . . .")

Tom had tuned out quickly. But he was kept from nodding off — another habit of his — by the discomfort of the government-issue chairs on which he and the G-man faced each other across a table, and by his fascination with a birthmark on Agent Bronowski's scalp. Clearly visible through the man's thinning hair, it looked so strikingly like the outline of a tiny barbershop quartet that it was all Tom could do to resist tracing over it with his fountain pen.

Agent Bronowski did eventually get to the point in the second hour, although he was just as circumlocutory as he'd been while gushing over Tom in the first.

("I'm confident you spontaneously analyzed the nature of the investigations that originate in this office . . .") Tom had indeed made a note of the sign on the door: Federal Bureau of Investigation — National Security.

("It's your work, Doctor Jones, in, in — this is terribly awkward — I believe the word is polyesters? Our interest is in that. Well, it's not quite that simple.") Tom had remained entirely expressionless, letting Bronowski lead.

("As you know, with war almost certain in Europe, and, well, with your company's rather close relationship with the industrialists of the Third Reich, I, ah, well in a nutshell, what we need from you, ah, what your country needs from you is, well, what you are doing with this, this new polyester formula.")

The interview ended not long after that, with Tom agreeing to meet Agent Bronowski again in two days after thinking over what he'd been asked. When he'd prepared for bed that night, setting out his blue uniform as he always did, the one with the Janitorial Services tag over the pocket, the issue of balance did not occur to him immediately. He was more preoccupied with how the FBI could have confused him with the other Tom Jones, one of the company's research chemists. It was only when he realized that the whole thing was a set-up — that particular insight came the next morning — that the idea of balance came to him as well. What he would do, he decided, was speak to the real FBI. The agency would be quite interested, he was sure, in doing a little balancing of its own.

Why does Tom Jones know that his interview was a set-up?

27

Paying Attention
to Esme Quartz

IT WAS NOT UNTIL AFTER THE JURY had returned a guilty verdict without even retiring to deliberate, that detectives at the 17th Precinct acknowledged MaryPat St. Martin's role on the day of the shooting. She had been the only one in the station on that extremely busy day to pay any attention to the woman who turned out to be the prosecution's star witness.

Not that a reasonable person would point a finger of blame at the others for this. The witness, Esme Quartz, was well known to the 17th, and everyone in the station, MaryPat included, did what they could to avoid her. With her chin pulled back and her mouth fixed in a pucker of disgust, Esme conveyed the impression that at a very early age she had stepped in a dog turd and decided then and there that life was never going to get any better and, if it was going to be that way, then others were going to share her misery.

At least once a month, the 17th had to deal with a complaint either by or about Esme. She warred with her fellow tenants in the old brownstone just blocks from the station. She seemed unable to complete even the simplest transaction in the little stores that lined her street without getting into shouting matches with the owners. Even her dog (and only friend), along with her several cats, shared her sour disposition and was yet another source of agony for the beleaguered cops. Perhaps worst of all was Esme's paranoia. Her conviction that everyone around her — neighbors, strangers, service people, even the police — was out to cheat, maim, and steal was unshakable. It was no surprise, therefore, when she appeared at the duty sergeant's desk on that rainy day, before the shooting scene had even been secured. And when she announced in her clipped tones that she knew not only who the shooter was but where to find him, only MaryPat had bothered to look up.

The shooting had been one of those big-city crimes that make police and civilians alike shudder in the awareness of how helpless both can be in the face of random violence. It came at the end of a day and a half of steady rain that seemed to push the city into a frenzy of aggressive crime, taxing the 17th to its limits. A male in his thirties had walked out of a movie theater into the middle of the street, taken out a gun, and begun to fire into the crowd sheltering under the theater's marquee. He then escaped the carnage he'd created by running over the roofs of cars and disappearing into a subway tunnel.

As though to reinforce the kind of day the 17th was having, no fewer than eleven 9-1-1 calls reported the incident within five minutes of the shooting, despite the fact that the streets were empty because of the rain. Yet not one witness had been found who could provide a reliable and credible description of the gunman. Except, as it turned out, for Esme.

Less than an hour after the first 9-1-1 call, Esme planted herself in front of the duty sergeant's desk and bleated for attention. Her physical appearance that day, while typical, seemed to symbolize the chaos in the station. One shoe had no heel. Her coat was misbuttoned and ringed at the bottom with dog hair. It was also soaking wet, and dripped a steady stream onto the tile, making it slippery and dangerous. Sheets of the newspaper she'd held over her head gradually parted company with one another as she made tentative grabs at the detectives who ventured near her.

Only MaryPat had stopped. What she learned by stopping to listen led to an arrest, charge, conviction, and sentence. Still, Esme's reputation had jeopardized the outcome even after MaryPat had the name and address of the shooter, for when she took the information to the precinct commander, his immediate response was to dismiss it, pointing out to MaryPat that no one, not even a nutcase like Esme Quartz, would have been out on the street in that heavy rain. Esme, he said pointedly, had walked down to the station because she smelled disaster and wanted to enjoy it, and that was how she'd gotten wet.

Only after MaryPat insisted did the commander realize that Esme just might be a genuine witness.

How did MaryPat St. Martin know that Esme Quartz had a reason to be on the street in the rain, and therefore just might have seen the shooting?

28

Investigating the Failed Drug Bust

THERE WAS STILL A BIT OF SNOW on the ground, small piles of it wrapped around the base of the trees that lined both sides of the path. There was even more of it just a few feet off the path where, years before, the Department of Parks and Recreation had made yet another attempt to create the illusion of a natural environment in the middle of the city. Betty Stadler rather enjoyed the irony of it all. The trees grew and the snow fell, and every winter weekend enthusiastic urbanites, dressed better than Scott's polar expedition, pretended they were confronting the forces of nature — without ever straying off the path.

Still, phony as it was, Gallenkirk Park was better than no park at all. A lot better. And Betty Stadler, Lieutenant Elizabeth Stadler, recently appointed to Internal Affairs, had to admit she preferred to be out here, especially if the alternative was another smoke-filled committee room back at headquarters. Years before, more years than she cared to acknowledge, when she was the force's first female officer, Gallenkirk Park had been in her precinct. She had been part of an experimental bicycle patrol group that covered the park, along with an adjacent public housing project that had been put together during the Eisenhower administration with a lot less planning than Parks and Rec had put into the trees.

She'd loved the park then, and did even more so now. The trees were mature now, and had attracted some wildlife. There was irony in that too. Nature, "red in tooth and claw," as Tennyson had put it, had returned to the middle of the city. But the fauna was far less dangerous than the wildlife that dominated the drug trade in the high-rise projects next door, a trade that contaminated everyone and everything that came into even the remotest contact with it.

Betty was acutely aware of the ultimate irony in her situation this morning. She was here in one of her favorite places in the whole city, but only because it might provide a setting for one of her least favorite responsibilities: investigating whether a cop might be dirty.

Not a rookie this time, not like the last time when her investigation turned up a scandalous mess that traced back to the police academy. The one this time was an officer with some fifteen years' tenure. He had spent the last three years undercover on the "old clothes" detail, living in shelters and on the street, soaking up information and cheap wine. In a way she felt sorry for the cops on "old clothes." They volunteered for it all right; no one forced them, even though it could be a real career boost because it was one of those ugly but very important police jobs that few wanted. But so many of the personnel on this detail eventually developed a real problem staying level. Either they became fanatics, crusaders, so that Betty and her team ended up investigating them for unnecessary force or illegal entrapment, or else they became so soiled by the world they dealt with that they became part of it.

Betty had met Officer Dana only once before. He'd been a member of the mounted patrol then, a coveted assignment, and she couldn't understand why he'd volunteered to transfer out. It could have been the divorce, she thought when reading his file. The break-up had been messy, and for Dana, excruciating. His two kids now lived with their mother over a thousand miles away. Yet the shift to "old clothes" seemed to be the right thing to do, at least in the beginning. In his first year he'd turned over enough good stuff to earn three citations. But his markers slowed after that, and in the third year his file showed such a sharp decline that Internal Affairs had flagged it. A few hours ago that attention had made Betty notice something in the morning reports that, most times, would have slid through without even a raised eyebrow.

The night before, the narcotics squad had pulled off a major bust that was coordinated across several points in the city. It had taken months of preparation, and although the squad had proceeded with its customary secrecy and, in Betty's opinion, utter lack of cooperation from the rest of the force, it was impossible to hide the fact that something big was going down. By the time of the bust, the where and when, and even the who, were common knowledge. Even so, the squad went ahead with every expectation of success and everything went as planned, except for one small and, on the surface, entirely peripheral part: a failed arrest in Gallenkirk Park. The only collar the squad made there was a wino who so far had refused to talk.

According to the detective from narcotics — he was the only one who saw it firsthand, other than Dana and the drug dealers who had gotten away — the potential collars had been approaching from three different directions for their meet. When they were almost within speaking distance of one another, the sound of someone walking through the leaves just off the path tipped them off. Although it was too dark to see much, the dealers were taking no chances and scattered. The approaching person, the one who scared them off, turned out to be just a wino, but by then the operation was dead. The wino, who Betty knew to be Officer Dana, had been charged with obstructing police business. It was a sour-grapes charge at best and, if the stories all checked out, one that would be dropped quickly to save everyone embarrassment.

Had Betty not come out here this morning to confirm her suspicions, it all might have ended there, but now she knew there was dirt. More than she'd originally suspected, because now there were two cops to investigate.

She took a deep breath, and turned completely around for a last long look. She was sure she'd seen a robin at the top of an oak tree just ahead. An early returner, but a good sign. Further ahead she saw the sun trying to push its way through the clouds. Another good sign. After a week of almost steady drizzle and gloom, some sunshine would be welcome.

Why has Lieutenant Betty Stadler determined that there are now two cops to investigate?

29

A Surprise Witness
for the Highland
Press Case

NORMALLY, JANE FORRESTER DIDN'T WASTE her time even thinking about buying a lottery ticket. The logic of such a move, given the odds of winning, had always eluded her. It was only after she left The Toby Jug, the day before Christmas, that Jane gave the idea serious consideration for the very first time. Standing there in the parking lot, digging in her purse for her car keys, it occurred to her that she might well be on a streak of good luck.

First, there was the matter of bumping into Wally Birks. Well, not just bumping; she'd walked right into him. Almost knocked him over. She'd been heading for the one empty stool at the bar in The Toby Jug, then suddenly changed her mind and walked to the back to use the washroom. With her thoughts on trying to identify just which one of the patrons was Wally Birks, she crashed into the back of a man in a blue parka who'd stopped suddenly at the entrance to the little alcove. Directly ahead a bright red door said "Private." On the left wall was the "Ladies" door, and opposite it the "Gents." Both in bright red.

Funny how she remembered the colors: the red doors and

his blue parka, and the truly ugly carpeting. Ocher. Who on earth picks ocher?

Probably the colors stuck because of the phone call just before noon.

"You're Forrester, they tell me, Jane Forrester?" a gravelly and very pedantic voice had asked. "Well, I'm Birks, Wally Birks. That's Walter of course, but the only one ever called me Walter was my mother, and actually, she's been dead now, oh, some twenty years. Even my teachers never called me Walter —"

"Sir!" Jane broke in before she got a life history complete with favorite foods. "You wanted to speak to me about something, sir?"

"Well, actually . . . yes. You see, I've been sitting here thinking. Got lots of time to do that now. Actually, I'm retired, you see, and —"

"Sir! Could you tell me what it is you wanted to speak about?" Jane tried to keep the edge out of her voice.

"OK. Yes. Right. Sure. The Highland Press thing. Outside The Toby Jug? That's my favorite pub. And I saw something . . . Well, actually, I should have called you before this, but you see, a person doesn't always want to get involved, now, does he? And I was thinking . . . Matter of fact, I was just saying to my brother-in-law the other day . . ."

Despite herself, Jane held off interrupting. The Highland Press case was one of the open files on her desk, and every lead had been exhausted. Only a plum like a surprise witness was going to give her a break.

". . . so I was thinking, actually, I should meet you there. At the pub?"

Jane took a deep breath. "Yes, sir. That sounds like a good idea. Could we meet this afternoon?"

"Actually, I was just going to suggest that. I'll be there wearing a grey parka so you'll know who I am. It's got a nice black fur trim on the hood. My daughter and son-in-law gave it to me for Christmas two years ago. They live —"

"Mr. Birks, can you be there at three o'clock?"

"Well, now, I suppose I could. You see, the pub's right on the way to —"

"That's great, Mr. Birks. See you then. Bye for now."

Between the time of that call and her visit to The Toby Jug, Jane Forrester tried without success to put Wally Birks out of her mind. It was obvious he was the kind of person who could make the Charge of the Light Brigade sound like instructions for repotting azaleas, but the Highland Press case was a stickler, and if he could help, then . . .

As it turned out, Jane's time at the pub was mercifully brief. When she apologized to the man in the blue parka, he turned around very slowly.

"Now, I recognize that voice, don't I, Jane Forrester? Actually, I was wondering how we'd meet. This is a pretty big place. And busy. I have to go in there, you see." With his thumb he pointed over his shoulder at the doors. "At my age, a person has to, well, I don't want to talk about that to a lady. But you see, the thing is, I don't have my grey parka on like I told you I would. You'd never guess what happened. I went out to the back porch to get it. You see, before my wife got sick we had the porch closed in. She always called it 'the sun room' after that. I could never get used to that. A porch is a porch, I always say."

At that very moment, another piece of good luck happened. Jane's beeper screamed at her, and even before she'd scanned for the number, she was saying, "Oh, Mr. Birks. I'm so dreadfully sorry. An emergency. Look, I have to go. Now, someone from my office will call you for your information. It won't be me. One of my colleagues."

With that, she'd spun on her heels and disappeared before Wally Birks could wind up again.

Three bits of luck, she thought to herself in the parking lot, each saving her from wasting time with Wally Birks on the Highland Press case. Definitely worth considering a lottery ticket.

Jane Forrester's accidental bump, and her beeper sounding, are two bits of good luck. The third is the clue that tells her Wally is likely not a reliable informant, for he's already lied to her once. What is that lie?

30

The Last Will and
Testament of
Albion Mulmur

"IT TAKES ALL KINDS, MS. MACDUFFEE. Forgive me for
using such a worn cliché, but there are times when a platitude
can be surprisingly appropriate."

The words of the chief interviewer still resonated in Kay
MacDuffee's memory.

"According to these aptitude tests, you're really a poet at
heart," he'd said, "and I'm sure you'll agree that poets don't
make terribly good trial lawyers. Here at Finnerty, Coolihan
and Gore, that's what we specialize in: trials."

He'd paused — another image clearly etched in Kay's
memory — and puffed on an enormous cigar.

"But somehow," he went on, "I have a sense that you
could be very valuable in our investigation branch. Poets feel
things, and they can see better. I'm sure you know what I
mean . . ."

That was eighteen years ago, and over that time, Kay
MacDuffee's poetic insights had turned her into Finnerty,
Coolihan and Gore's star investigator. Those skills were serving her at this very moment, in the case of Albion Mulmur's
last will and testament, skills which had now convinced her

that old Mulmur's granddaughter, Regina, was attempting a neat piece of fraud.

Kay was sitting in what had been the old man's harness shop, relishing the soft smells of old leather, neat's-foot oil, and pipe tobacco which had worked their way into the wooden floors and walls, and into the naked pine beams supporting a loft where no one had climbed in years. She twisted in her seat, her eyes working in the gloom to pick up every nuance, imagining the stories that might emerge through the dust covering every one of the harness-making tools. She thought of what it must have been like to be a child in here, to lie in the loft and look down to watch Albion Mulmur turn rolls of leather into bridles and traces and cruppers.

It was a poet's room all right, one that appealed to the soul far more than the body. A dark place where, in winter, you chose between baking and freezing, depending on how close you pulled one of the old buggy seats to the potbellied stove; a place where the door hinges were so worn with use that unless it was given a shove to force the latch into place, the door would open ever so slowly, gathering momentum as it responded to the slant in the floor. It was the kind of place where the dirt, well, the dirt just belonged. To sweep or dust would have been almost an act of violence.

By itself the harness shop did little to support the notion that the old man's will could possibly require anything remotely resembling an investigation. But in 1938 Albion Mulmur, in an act regarded by those around him as one of sheer insanity, had purchased a thousand shares of IBM stock. Right now the original certificates and Mulmur's signed and duly witnessed will were safely stowed at the offices of Finnerty, Coolihan and Gore, along with letters, not yet mailed, from a senior partner advising various charities that they were the beneficiaries of several million dollars.

The letters had been held up because another will with a later date had been found in the harness shop by one of the firm's law clerks. This will left all but ten percent of Albion

Mulmur's estate to his only grandchild, Regina.

Kay's meeting with Regina — the granddaughter had left about half an hour before — had almost ruined her experience of the harness shop. She had arrived early and was only just beginning to bask in the place when Regina came — intruded, as far as Kay was concerned. The shop seemed to demand quiet and patience, and measured, deliberate movements. Regina, however, literally blew in.

"Gawd! I haven't been here since I was a little kid!" she said, a look of self-conscious disbelief on her face. "Almost used to live in here then! Can you imagine?" She pushed the door closed with one shoulder. "Still stinks of those pipes, doesn't it? And the dirt. Gawd, my mother hated the dirt. And the cobwebs. They're thicker than ever!"

With a gloved hand she repositioned a pair of designer frames to the bridge of a very long nose, then assessed Kay in an unabashed stare.

"Sorry I'm late. How long you been here? Aren't you cold?" Without waiting for an answer, Regina looked away from Kay and grimaced as she looked up at the loft.

"Hasn't changed in twenty years. You don't mind if I stand, do you? Those buggy seats — you sure you want to sit there? There's probably something living in them, you know!"

The interview wasn't really an interview, Kay reflected later; Regina Mulmur had delivered a monologue that had lasted about fifteen minutes, and then departed in the same style she'd entered. Still, for Kay it was long enough. She was more than happy when Regina left, for it meant Kay would be able to return to her enjoyment of the place. Besides, she was convinced now that the recently discovered will was definitely a phony one.

What has convinced Kay MacDuffee that the newly discovered will is likely fraudulent?

31

What Happens in
Scene Three?

SCENE ONE

(Dark stage except for a small area lit by a single spot upper right. The edges of the spot vaguely pick up the sitting room of a gentlemen's club. Center of the spot, in a leather easy chair, facing stage right is a man with elegant silver hair. There is no reason to conclude he is old: just dignified, and apparently wealthy. The light, in any case, is not strong enough to reveal other than hazy details. What is clear, however, is the white, business-size envelope in his left hand, stuffed to the maximum and secured with cellulose tape. The man holds what may be a glass of wine, or more likely sherry, in the other hand. His legs are crossed at the ankles, underneath a small, rectangular coffee table.

The man on the other side of this table is standing, so that his face is above the light. He is wearing a three-piece suit, gray pinstripe. Over a slight but visible paunch, a gold watch chain loops across his vest.

No dialogue is heard in this scene, but over its twenty or so seconds' duration, it is apparent that the man in the chair is talking, for his hands move in a gesticulatory fashion. In the final seconds, he places the envelope on the coffee table. The other man picks it up slowly. His right hand lingers at the table long enough for his ring to be obvious. The principal stone is a large ruby set in a circle of diamonds.

Start chamber music just before he picks up the envelope. Bring up music; fade to black, and hold music into Scene Two.

SCENE TWO

Almost immediately, a spot comes up downstage from Scene One, and somewhat stage left. The lit-up area is larger this time, but still does not pick up walls or anything that might suggest the confines of the stage.

The gray-suited man from Scene One is now standing in front of a small bar in a luxuriously appointed private library. He's facing slightly stage left, because the bar runs upstage-downstage. The watch chain and ruby ring clearly identify him, but again his face is above the light. This time, he is holding a gun with a silencer on the barrel.

The weapon is casually pointed at GEORGE FEWSTER, standing behind the bar. He's shorter than the gunman [*Note: If necessary, use altered stage floor levels to show height differential.*] and unlike the gunman, his face can be seen. FEWSTER's mustache and hair are streaked with gray. He's wearing a smoking jacket, and has just poured a drink which he places on the bar. Fade music but hold softly throughout.)

GUNMAN: You're not joining me?

FEWSTER: Hardly a celebratory occasion, wouldn't you say?

GUNMAN: Depends on your point of view, Mr. Fewster. Now, your partner, I'm sure, is quite likely enjoying a libation or two, in anticipation of the outcome of this, ah, how shall I say, event?

FEWSTER: What I don't understand is, why didn't you just shoot me when I came into the library? That's what you've been paid to do. Why prolong the matter? Or is this some sort of perverse pleasure you have arranged for yourself?

GUNMAN: Perverse, Mr. Fewster? Surely not perverse. No, I see it as an exploration — how shall I call it? — a probing into the human spirit.

FEWSTER: You want to see how I conduct myself, knowing that I'm about to be, er . . .

GUNMAN: Precisely!

FEWSTER: . . . perhaps to see what steps I'll take to thwart you.

GUNMAN: Oh really, Mr. Fewster! A man of your perspicacity! Thwart me? I really do know how to use this weapon. It has served me well. And you must have deduced by now, that inasmuch as I knew the balcony doors were not locked, I also know you are alone tonight. The silencer is merely a precaution. And the drink here? Now that was just a trifle amateur, Mr. Fewster. When I leave, I'll take it with me. DNA and all that. It is good Scotch, nevertheless. A single malt, I assume. A bit peaty for my taste, but elegant.

FEWSTER: So the conclusion here is foregone, in your opinion.

GUNMAN: Oh, without question. It's only an issue now of assessing how you approach the inevitability of it.

FEWSTER: I see.
  (*In a very natural move, and without looking up to note the gunman's quick flinch, Fewster reaches under the bar for the Scotch and*

pours himself a drink. Then he looks up.)
  Changed my mind. A legitimate, last-minute prerogative, I'm sure you'll agree. By the way, have you ever given thought to examining your own motivations, Mr. . . .

GUNMAN: Smith will do.

FEWSTER: It usually does.

GUNMAN: When you say "motivations," surely you're not thinking of some trite concept like morality or ethics?

FEWSTER: Actually, I was thinking of something a touch more fundamental. Like greed.
  (*Other than the reaction seconds before, the gunman has not moved until this point. Now he rotates slowly left then right, but only a few degrees.*)

GUNMAN: A reasonable ploy, sir. You were thinking of offering me a better proposition than your partner has, perhaps one of the paintings in here? I did recognize a Corot in the hallway, and a Monet.

FEWSTER: There's a Picasso in the foyer.

GUNMAN: Indeed! A Picasso! Tempting! But, you see, I lead such a peripatetic lifestyle that, well, portability is essential. Liquidity even more so. I'm sure you understand. It's a disadvantage in my calling. Now, your partner. He would be the one to listen to such an offer, wouldn't he? A most greedy man, as you have apparently discovered. It's why he can't afford to let you live.

FEWSTER: No doubt he's given you cash.

GUNMAN: A commodity for which there is no substitute.

FEWSTER: Not even my Fabergé eggs? Look at "The Peacock" here. Made for the Dowager Empress Maria in 1908.

(This time the gunman does not move as Fewster reaches unhesitatingly toward a glass case at the end of the bar and removes one of several very ornate eggs. Whether it is genuine, or a replica of one of the famous bejeweled eggs made for the Russian royal family by Peter Carl Fabergé, it is incredibly beautiful.)

GUNMAN: I must admit, sir, I did allow myself to examine them before you came in. Jewelry is one of my very few . . . They are especially exquisite, aren't they? I, er, I've always wanted to hold one of them. I — goodness!

(Fewster tosses the egg to the gunman, who catches it instinctively with his free hand. He raises the gun at Fewster slightly and, for what seems like an inordinately long time, examines the egg from every angle before handing it back.)

A sore temptation, I admit. And I do confess to an extraordinary fondness for precious stones. But then, surely you realize I could just avail myself in any case, after we conclude here?

(As Fewster delivers his next line, he turns to a wall safe behind him and opens it. The gun rises only slightly.)

FEWSTER: The truly beautiful ones in my collection are in the safe here.

GUNMAN: Indeed? Perhaps there's time — WHAT ARE YOU DOING?

(Continuing the fluid motion that opened the door to the safe, George Fewster sets the Peacock inside, closes the door, and twirls the dial.)

That was regrettable, Mr. Fewster! Almost juvenile! I'm surprised. Now open the safe, or I'm afraid I will have to fulfill my contract immediately!

FEWSTER: Come, come, Mr. Smith. Such impulsivity in a

student of human behavior! If you shoot now, you'll be missing a potentially inspiring opportunity.

GUNMAN: To what?
 (Fewster holds his drink to the light, and examines it.)

FEWSTER: To analyze your behavior over the next hour. After all, the outcome of this, er, event, is foregone, isn't it? At the very least, you might try to examine your motivations as it proceeds. It's just short of ten. I believe my partner's club is open till eleven.
 (Immediate fade to black.)

SCENE THREE

From the gunman's perspective, and George Fewster's too, there is only one way now that Scene Three can play out and bring this issue to a final close. What is that?

32

Almost an Ideal Spot for Breakfast

HE WAS RESPONDING TO A BURGLAR ALARM RELAY, but the first thing to cross Laurie Silverberg's mind as he led the way through the front door of the house and into the solarium on the left was what a wonderful place this would be to have breakfast each morning. The east wall faced the lake and, although all he could see on it now was ice, the view was still awe inspiring. The wall was completely windowed except for a sliding door at the extreme right end. Right now, the door was open ever so slightly — jimmied — which was almost for sure what had made the alarm go off.

Laurie lingered in the entrance so he could get a full perspective of the room. This was a legitimate move from an investigative point of view, especially given that the three officers who had arrived with him were now doing a room-by-room in the rest of the house. But what he really wanted to do was enjoy the solarium. The east view was certainly the choice one, for the north faced the road and was draped, and the south was shaded by a thick stand of spruce. The west wall, where he was standing, the wall that connected to the house, was bookshelved from top to bottom. He liked that.

But the books were very much outnumbered by expensive-looking objets d'art, mostly soapstone carvings. Laurie pressed one of the three wall switches beside him and instantly spot lighting illuminated the pieces and held them in flattering circles of soft glow.

"Thought so," he muttered, and then added, "Let's see . . ." and pressed another. From hidden speakers Vivaldi's *Four Seasons* filled the solarium. This time Laurie nodded, as though he'd just won a bet with himself. When the third switch didn't produce any result he was curious, but soon forgot about it. There was so much more to look at.

Across the room there were more books, all leather-bound these, and filling a shelf that ran the length of the wall beneath an impressive array of foliage. Variegated pothos, dieffenbachia, anthuriums, peace lilies, a most luxurious Princess philodendron, and several nephthytis stood side by side on the window shelf, their broad leaves open toward him like hands offering a blessing. Someone here really cared about plants.

"More than reading if I'm any judge," Laurie said to himself. He glanced quickly over his shoulder and crossed to the books where, beneath the trailing fronds of a Boston fern, gold lettering proudly announced a copy of Dante's *Divina Commedia*. He pulled it out and opened it, smiling with more than a little satisfaction at the sound of the crack. Two more books on the same shelf, *Selections from the Romantic Poets* and Voltaire's *Candide*, made the same sound. It made Laurie's grin widen.

"Hey! Can I come in now or what? It's my house!"

Laurie jumped to his feet. He'd forgotten Eugenia Melch, forgotten that in life all good things have compensations, for in this house she would come with breakfast.

"Your men are out front already! They say there's nobody in the house!" Eugenia spoke at parade ground level. It made Laurie retreat. "Didn't think there would be! Probably miles away by now! Oh, my babies!" She ran to the plants. "It's

OK, darlings! Momma's home now to look after you."

Eugenia's composure softened as she visited each plant along the windows, stroking some, putting her face into others, here and there adjusting the position of a pot just a tiny bit. Until she reached the sliding door.

"Aha! Right there, eh? The door! Got in that way, did they? Well, least the alarm still works! That's something. OK, what now? Don't you have to get fingerprints or something like that? Or take pictures? Hardly the time for reading, is it?"

Laurie had forgotten he was holding *Candide* in one hand and the Romantic poets in the other. His voice, naturally soft, invariably got softer when confronted by a barrage like the one Eugenia had just laid down, so he almost whispered a response.

"I think the first thing we should do is go through the house together to see what's missing, if anything. Certainly this room seems to be intact."

"Is that so? Well, you could be right!"

Eugenia Melch accelerated around the room, examining the carvings. Her massive earrings flashed each time she came to a lighted spot and geared down for a second or two before passing to the next.

"All Sully's soap stuff is here, looks like!"

She talked as she went. Laurie watched her, fascinated by the earrings, wondering if they could be used to locate hidden radio transmitters.

"What he pays for this stuff! You can't imagine! And he can't even say their names, the people that do it! They're Eskimos, you know!" She shook her head. "Anyway, I can't see anything missing. Sully might, though, when he gets here."

Laurie did whisper this time. "Where is he, Mrs. Melch?"

"At his office. I dropped him off. We've been at the condo for the past week, and we —"

She noticed Laurie's slight frown. "In Nassau! The condo. The condo's in Nassau! That's what you're frowning about, isn't it? Anyway, we just got back a couple hours ago. Tickets are here in my purse if you want to see 'em. Or maybe Sully's got 'em. Anyway, he wanted to go to the office first so I dropped him and came home. I could hear the alarm when I came up the drive so I stayed in the car till you guys came. We had one a' these once before and the cop that time said nobody should ever go in, so I didn't! So now what? You want to go over the rest of the house?"

"If you think this room is accounted for, yes."

Laurie Silverberg and Eugenia Melch went through the entire house and found no other points of forced entry, and as well, found nothing missing as they went. It was not until they reached the master bedroom that Eugenia discovered that her diamond tiara, with matching necklace, brooch, rings, and bracelet, had been taken. By then, though, Laurie had determined that if anything were to turn up missing, it would be a case of fraud, not theft. Why?

33

Investigating
the Explosion

"THERE." MARNI RAINTZ POINTED to the markings inked onto a large piece of plate glass, being careful not to touch them. "Right there," she said. "Now that's a swastika, isn't it? Or most of one anyway. I bet we'll find the one little piece of missing line when we find the rest of the door."

Doug Doyle nudged the glass ever so slightly with the toe of one of his gleaming Oxfords. He was the only member of the bomb squad who never wore sneakers or construction boots, and he was famous for being able to crawl around an explosion site for days without ever having to rehabilitate a shoeshine. Doug looked at the markings and wrinkled his nose slightly. He didn't appear convinced.

"And here." Marni pointed at some more marks a few inches above the swastika. "This looks like it was probably another one, but it got smeared by the sprinkler system."

She bent at the knees and squatted closer to the wreckage lying between her and Doug. There were three pieces of glass from the shattered front door, each about the size of a large dinner plate. Two of them still clung, one beside the other, to one side of the wooden door frame, directly above the door knob. The third one was very slightly larger, and attached to a different piece of frame. This third one had the swastika. The blast had been a fairly small one, taking out the ornate front door of a large private home, and much of the outside living room wall on one side, along with a piece of the garage on the other side. "Looks very professional," the fire chief had said to Doug Doyle when he arrived a few minutes ago. "As if it's a message, sort of. Most of the force appears to have been horizontal. Very controlled. Could have been a lot worse."

Marni stood up and drew her shoulders back to stretch them, waiting for Doug to comment. He was staring at the glass. The swastika, if indeed it was one, was about the size of an adult's hand, and had been drawn with magic marker or some kind of felt-tip pen. Freehand and hastily too. Doug took a sharp breath as though he was about to say something, but instead held his breath and then exhaled slowly. Marni spoke instead.

"What I want to know is if you're thinking what I'm thinking. I mean, this was a real professional pop here. Whoever did this knew what he was doing with plastic. It was plastic, by the way, as if you couldn't tell first thing. And then the swastika . . . I mean, on first impression it's hard to get around the idea that some Nazi types were busy here."

Marni squatted down again and motioned Doug to do likewise. "But now look at what doesn't make any sense." She took out a ballpoint pen and with the blunt end drew a circle on the glass, around the swastika, as though to confine the symbol permanently to that one spot. "What doesn't seem to make sense," she went on, "is that the arms bend the wrong way on this thing. Isn't a swastika supposed to go clockwise? The ends of the arms, I mean? These are counterclockwise."

Doug spoke for the first time. "Is all the photography finished?" he said.

Marni nodded, just a bit perplexed.

"Then try this perspective," Doug Doyle said gently as he

picked up the piece of glass and turned it over. "Now it's clockwise, right? The way it's supposed to be?"

Marni reddened, but before she could say anything, Doug set the glass down and touched her elbow so that both of them would stand up.

"The fact is," he said, "swastikas can go either way, clockwise or counterclockwise. When Hitler adopted the symbol, he picked the former direction." Doug looked at his young colleague. Her interest appeared genuine, so he continued. "It's a very ancient symbol, really, and quite widespread. The Hindu and Buddhist traditions have it. You would have found it in Mexico too, long before the Europeans came. Ever heard of Heinrich Schliemann, the guy that found Troy in the 1870s? He also found swastikas there. I believe he was the first to refer to them as an Aryan religious symbol, although there's no evidence that Schliemann himself was a racist."

Marni was listening intently, but by now Doug was on a roll and her interest no longer made much difference.

"Actually, it's generally believed that swastikas were intended to have a benign purpose. To represent the motion of the sun, most archeologists think. It's only after Hitler that the swastika became tainted, culturally."

Doug squatted down and, just as Marni had done, traced a circle around the swastika on the glass with the blunt end of his ballpoint pen. He continued, without changing his tone even a little.

"There's an interesting legend about the Crusaders and the swastika. The story has it that they were laying siege to a fortress — somewhere in the Middle East, I don't know where — and as a ploy the inhabitants had their women place their bare butts over the edge of the fortress wall, just to show the brave knights how much they cared about the siege. And all the bottoms had swastikas painted on them."

For the first time, Marni's expression changed. Doug's didn't. He kept on staring at the swastika.

"I'm not making that up," he added. "There really is such a story. But anybody who believes that would also believe that some Nazi types are responsible for this bomb blast here."

Why does Doug Doyle suspect that this explosion was not set by what he and Marni call "Nazi types"?

34

Some Uncertainty about the Call at 291 Bristol

THERE WERE AT LEAST THREE GOOD REASONS why Shaun Hawkes was not prepared to accept the incident at 291 Bristol as a break and enter. Not as a robbery either, or an assault, even though all that had to be put aside for the moment while she looked after the young woman who'd called 9-1-1. Paige Kress was her name, eighteen years old and by all indications genuinely traumatized. In Shaun's mind it was a heck of a thing to happen to a young college kid on her Christmas break, so she was now puttering about the huge kitchen at 291 Bristol, looking for the wherewithal to brew a pot of tea, Shaun's standard response to trauma, illness, and global crisis.

"He was gonna, I was so scared he was gonna . . ." Paige's first words to Shaun degenerated into moans as she wrapped her arms around herself tightly and rocked back and forth.

"He was here before, the guy. Like, in the house . . ." had come through the tears. "See, we're gonna move . . . Daddy's company's got some kind of trouble . . . and he needs to . . . to . . ." Paige had begun to hyperventilate. That's when Shaun had left for the kitchen. She wanted to make some space for herself, and tea for all hands.

Two of the uniforms on her squad were sitting with Paige right now, one of them the only other female member of the squad, a veteran of all of six months who had been the first officer on the scene. This same rookie, a month before, had investigated a report of three girls being stalked on the campus of the junior college nearby. One of the three had been Paige Kress.

The third cupboard door to the left of the triple sink yielded an electric tea kettle. Progress.

"Add that to the milk," Shaun said aloud, "and the dubious contents of that sugar bowl, and we're getting somewhere. Now, what's needed is a nice Darjeeling or maybe a Pekoe."

The search went on. A second bank of cupboard doors presented an impressive array of serving dishes and baking tools but no tea, so she moved to the third. Actually, this was taking about as much time as she had hoped it would. Paige, in Shaun's opinion, needed some time before telling her story again. The first time, between the sobs and fits of quivering, and even a near-faint, Paige had told the officers how she had just stepped out of the shower when she heard — she was certain about this — she heard a sound in the hall. Wrapped in only a towel, Paige had peeked out the door, but saw nothing. It was when she had turned back inside that she saw the intruder in the mirror: a man, a short man, dressed all in black, carrying a painting. She'd screamed, locked the door, and called 9-1-1.

"Ah, gotcha!" Shaun's delight at finally finding some tea was short-lived. It was a herbal tea. Mint. In her opinion, that was as close to barbaric as one could get without resorting to coffee. This search for tea was becoming as bothersome as the case! Even the man in black had been easier to find.

Paige had identified him as the real-estate estimator who had been through the house the week before. He was now sitting in handcuffs in the back seat of a blue and white parked in the driveway. Shaun herself had picked him up only a block away.

She had to admit she disliked him immediately, probably because his black shirt was opened to mid-chest, revealing a cross on a gold chain, a St. Jude medal and, also in gold, a fist with middle finger raised in a rude gesture. He was short, dressed in black, and swaggery. Not Shaun's kind of person. Still, there had been no painting anywhere near; not that she'd expected to find one, even though the black Trans-Am where she'd picked him up was his. As well, his story that he'd returned to the neighborhood to re-evaluate his original estimate made sense enough. Paige's parents were selling their huge home and he'd been called in on the same day they were leaving for a week of skiing. His first go-round, he claimed, had been too rushed. The place needed a closer look, he went on. Too many things were not working: the garage-door opener, the burglar alarm, the garburetor. The house needed a thorough examination.

"Well," Shaun exclaimed as she opened and closed the very last cupboard door. "This is uncivilized! One cannot have a kitchen and not have tea! What do these people do for —"

With a look of chagrin on her face, she stopped and peeked over her shoulder to see if anyone had seen her search.

"Some detective!" she said, and walked to the sink. The set of canisters on the kitchen counter had labels clear enough to read from anywhere in the room: FLOUR, SUGAR, COFFEE, TEA. She peered out the kitchen door just to be doubly sure none of her squad had been nearby. Shaking her head in self-admonishment, she began to fill the kettle with water.

Shaun Hawkes almost overlooked the obvious in her search for tea, but she hasn't been fooled by this case. What are "at least three good reasons" why she is not prepared to accept this incident as break and enter, robbery, or assault?

35

The Case of
the Missing Child

THE TENSION BETWEEN THE COUPLE was like static electricity, ready to crackle at the first sign of movement. But from where Audrey Greenwood stood in the doorway, it didn't appear there was going to be any movement unless she initiated it. Downstairs, when she'd first come in, the couple had taken great care to avoid any contact with each other, like a pair of magnets carrying the same charge. Now it continued in the bedroom.

The father stood with his back to one of the windows, arms folded tightly across his chest, the old-fashioned venetian blinds framing his rigid vertical stance. Audrey felt that this corner room was ideal for the tableau inside, for the mother stood equally erect at the window on the south wall. She, however, held her arms akimbo and was staring resolutely out the window into the apartments across the street.

As it turned out, the tension had an ultimate benefit in the case, for its force made Audrey pause longer in the doorway than she otherwise might have. Normally, in cases like this, when she was first to arrive, she would assert herself quickly so that no matter which way headquarters decided to play it, the victims involved would see her as the principal investigator. Audrey worked out of Juvenile Branch, a more effective group, in her opinion, than the stumblebums from Felonious Crimes, one of whom would arrive shortly. On the surface, the issue was either a kidnapping with, quite possibly, murder involved, or a simple runaway.

The room where the two parents stood braced for combat was a child's bedroom in metamorphosis from nursery to little-girl sanctuary. There was a diaper-changing table along the wall the father was facing, but, covered in Barbie Doll paraphernalia, it seemed to have outgrown its original purpose. The bed on the fourth wall had only recently been a crib, but the sides were gone now. Only the wallpaper, a rigorously gender-balanced mix of pink and blue cherubs, obviously chosen before the child's birth, had survived the change so far.

The crayon marks on the wallpaper were the first indication to Audrey that there might be something different about this child. There were just too many of them. They were too random, too thick. Then there was the tiny shelf near the ceiling. Way too high and out of reach to be normally functional, it was clearly purpose-built. An empty pharmacy bottle suggested what it had once been used for. Other things begged to be explained too, especially the nails in the window frames. Like the blinds, the windows were old, this being one of three late-Depression-era buildings holding out against a growing forest of new high-rise apartments. But the windows were nailed shut. Behind the father, Audrey could easily see the nails protruding from both frames.

"Lexie has a behavior disorder." Was the mother reading her mind? The voice continued through lips that barely moved. "The doctors don't know what it is. We've — No! *I've* taken her to, oh God, it seems like a hundred of them. She's got drugs, but they don't work. Sometimes I think they make her worse. She's a head-banger, she runs, she screams . . . I, oh God . . ."

For the first time, the mother's defenses seemed to weaken. Her shoulders drooped and brought her head down.

Out of experience, Audrey resisted any feelings of sympathy as she turned to the father. "This morning, when you first noticed she was missing . . ."

"It's happened a couple of times," he sighed. "Once we found her under the laundry tub, the other time in a broom closet. That's why we didn't call you right away. We searched the house first. When we couldn't find her —"

"Your call was logged at 7:44 A.M.," Audrey interrupted him. "When did you see her bed was empty?"

This time the woman spoke up. "My clock radio's set for 7:20. See, sometimes she sleeps in. It's rare but it happens, so just in case . . . She's got to have medication before eight or the day's pure hell. Anyway, Buzz got up when the radio went off, and he . . . well, when he couldn't find her he woke me up and we called 9-1-1."

Audrey nodded. "When did you last see her, then?"

"When she was put to bed last night," the father answered. "Just after eight. We both did it."

"The second time you've helped this month!" Her rigid stance had returned. "Don't tell me this is a trend!"

Audrey ignored the sarcasm and put her next question before the father could lay out the response she saw was coming. "Didn't either of you, er, before you went to bed yourselves . . ."

"Go in to check? Tuck her in?" The mother's posture had stiffened even more. "Lexie is not very tuckable. Once she's asleep, you don't take a chance on waking her up. Sometimes her day starts at midnight. Anything can set her off — light, unfamiliar noise, even the wrong cooking smell." She slumped noticeably. "Besides, I fell asleep in front of the TV." The slump got lower and her voice became a pleading whisper. "Look. You don't know how exhausting it is to have a child like Lexie. It never stops! I . . . I just fell asleep."

By now she could barely be heard. Audrey could see tears.

"That's right." It was the father. "I was out last night. My poker night. Once a month. It's the only night I ever have for myself. I got back — oh, it had to be about 1:30 — and she, er, Jean, she was asleep in the living room. The TV was on, so I turned it off and covered her with a blanket.

"Before you ask — No, I didn't go in to Lexie's room either. You soon learn around here that when it's quiet you leave well enough alone."

The doorbell rang, making all of them jump. Audrey's partner had arrived.

"What have you touched in here this morning?" Audrey asked hastily. "You know, what have —"

"When I came in with you just now," the mother interrupted, "that's the first time since last night when I — oh goodness — when *we* put her to bed."

"And you, sir?" Audrey looked at the father.

"Just opened the door," he said. "Came in a few steps, I guess. Looked under the bed, of course." He paused. "Well, you can see the covers are peeled right down. It was obvious Lexie wasn't in the bed."

Audrey nodded and stepped back down the hall a bit. "Up here!" she called. "But we're coming down." She motioned to the mother and father to follow her and then called downstairs again. "This one is yours!"

Audrey Greenwood has decided that this is not a juvenile crime, such as a runaway or a missing child, but a felony. What has led her to that decision?

36

A Clever Solution
at the County Fair

IT TOOK ONLY A COUPLE OF SECONDS for Chris Fogolin to realize that the change in his luck was holding. On the other side of the gently flapping canvas wall, the executive director of the Quail County Fair Board was shouting into the telephone. Chris could hear it as plainly as if J. Loudon Glint was talking to him directly.

"Who is this? Pincher? I thought so. Are you right there at the exhibit?" Glint was getting louder. The answer must have been affirmative for the next question was, "Well, can they hear you — Stipple and Two Feathers, I mean? Are they right there beside you, or . . . ?" There was the briefest of pauses and then a groan.

"Well, get private, for heaven sakes!" Glint was shouting now. "Why do you think we give you people cell phones! Honestly! . . . Yeah, yeah, yeah. Never mind that now! Look. Check your watch. Call me back in exactly one minute. On the inside line."

There was a slight thump and then a loud honk as J. Loudon Glint cleared his nasal tracks before shouting once more.

"Ellie! Bring me the entry forms on that homing pigeon exhibit! Right away!"

Ellie, who was also on the other side of the canvas wall, must have hesitated or looked perplexed because Glint came back immediately with, "Yes, all of them! There's only half a dozen entries in that class. I was down there this morning before the judging. Do I have to do everything myself?!"

Glint honked again. Twice. Chris was sympathetic. He too had a cold and wondered if that was what made the fair's executive director so cranky. Earlier that morning, Chris Fogolin had given serious thought to using his cold as an excuse to skip the county fair and stay in bed. His assignment was, all things considered, hardly the cutting edge of journalism. Chris was a crime reporter. Well, more accurately, that's what he wanted to be, but when one worked for the Quail County *Gleaner*, crime was limited to the police report on the second page, and most of that dealt with nothing more dramatic than stolen sheep. What would make the front page of *The Gleaner* tomorrow, and the day after, and the day after that, was news about the county fair. That more than anything else had gotten Chris out of bed. Better to have a by-line on the front page than no by-line at all.

Still, he'd spent the morning muttering under his breath about bad luck. Rain had begun to fall as soon as he entered the fair grounds. Bad for his cold and even worse for his shoes. Now there were not only cow patties to watch out for but mud too. And the rain had thinned the crowd, reducing the opportunity for a story. Even on *The Gleaner*, you had to have an angle to get on the front page.

But then the rain had brought good luck. A sudden downpour had driven Chris into the swine and fowl tent — he'd been walking past it, having decided well in advance to pretend it wasn't even there — and the first person he spotted was Madonna Two Feathers. She was always good for news. Madonna Two Feathers was an advocate for Native American rights, and known well beyond the borders of Quail County for her less than discreet methods. If Madonna Two Feathers was here, Chris knew, there had to be a story somewhere. Even if it was only a picture of her with her beloved pigeons. That, in fact, was something he did immediately: photograph Madonna Two Feathers sitting in her wheelchair holding a pair of pigeons in a cage on her lap. He then took a close-up of the identifying tag on the cage. "Cream Rollers," it said, obviously referring to the breed. Underneath the tag, a blue rosette with a pair of trailing blue ribbons proclaimed "FIRST PRIZE."

Chris Fogolin had been working in Quail County long enough to be aware that this was not some simple pet-raising venture. Madonna Two Feathers and her family were internationally famous among pigeon fanciers. A prize-winning pair of Cream Rollers could fetch thousands from the right buyer.

That knowledge had made Chris hang around after the pictures were taken to peer at some of the other Cream Rollers. After all, the rain was still coming down. There were five other pairs of pigeons in the exhibit. To Chris, they all looked exactly the same, making him wonder how the judges went about making a decision. Despite himself, he had leaned closer to the line of metal cages, and it was then that he found his story. The exhibitor right beside Madonna Two Feathers was Maxwell Stipple. Stipple was almost as well known as his neighboring exhibitor, but not for the kind of news *The Gleaner* liked to print. Stipple was a self-proclaimed white supremacist who, only three weeks before, had paid a huge fine for distributing anti–Native American slogans in front of the courthouse.

For Chris, the opportunity was a golden one. Even *The Gleaner* would like his angle: pigeons as the great leveler, the reason to set aside ill will and racist ideas in the clean spirit of competition. He'd immediately finished a roll of film on the spot, and then, forgetting entirely about the rain, dashed off to find Madonna Two Feathers again. Stipple too, if he could. That had been an hour ago. In his excitement he'd almost forgotten his editor's principal instruction: to photograph and interview the 4-H Grand Champion. A feature for that was already half written for today's edition. With that obligation to see to, he'd lost track of both Stipple and Two Feathers, and as a last resort he had decided to turn to J. Loudon Glint, who, if he was certain to be part of the story, would be sure to help.

The sound of Glint's telephone brought Chris back to the present.

"Pincher? Yeah. OK. Yeah, yeah . . . Oh, no! Oh my God, what next?" Glint wasn't shouting anymore, but he could still be heard very easily. An office in a tent just didn't make for privacy.

"Well, who spoke to you first, Stipple or Two Feathers? Yeah, yeah. And Stipple says they're his Cream Rollers, and she says they're hers? Yeah, I know. They all look the same to me too. And he's claiming that the first-prize ribbon was for his birds and she switched the name tags? Or maybe the ribbons? Oh, great! I think — just a minute."

Glint stopped to put out a tremendous honk.

"Now, look. I can't leave here right now. Hey, there's no press there, is there? Good. Now here's what you do. Here's the solution. What you do is take the . . ."

"Sir!" It was Ellie, her large nose pushing right into Chris's face. "You can't be here, sir! This is a restricted area. It's for employees of the fair board only. Now if you need shelter from the rain, we're more than happy to . . ."

Chris didn't stick around for the rest of it. It would take at least five minutes to get across the fair grounds to the exhibit where Pincher was about to follow Glint's instructions, and Chris wanted to get some shots of it.

Chris knows what Glint told Pincher to do, even though Ellie interrupted at the time, and he's going to photograph it for his paper. What has Glint told Pincher to do?

37

Even Birdwatchers Need to Watch Their Backs

RON MINAKER COULDN'T HELP BUT MARVEL at the trickle of water down the rock face at the other end of the bog. Hardly the Devil's Torrent, as it was described in brochures for the birdwatchers who traveled great distances to hike through the park and add to their lists.

"More like the Devil's Piddle," Ron said out loud to himself. "And this," he added, gesturing with his chin at the utterly still surface of the water, "this will soon be the Devil's Puddle if we don't get some rain."

He squatted down where the path forked, wincing at the cracking sound his knees made. At a slight angle to his left, the trail bent gracefully but precisely around the edge of the bog, bulged somewhat at the base of the waterfall where shifting feet had widened out a viewing space, and then disappeared into a stand of hardwoods. Above the hardwoods, a grove of cedars covered the face of the cliff from which the Devil's Torrent issued. The grove continued on over the rock face to the other side and petered out into hardwoods again. Ron couldn't see that latter part from where he was standing, but he had hiked it often enough to see it in his mind's eye.

The body of water was called McCarston's Lake on the map. A flattering description as far as Ron was concerned, even though there had always been water in it as far back as he could remember. Locals called it McCarston's Banana. That described its shape far more accurately. Still, government geologists had declared it a lake, and who was he to argue? Besides, he had more important things to consider this morning. Like the death of Jos Poot.

A birdwatcher, Jos Poot had been. At least, he'd been decked out in all the appropriate gear with all the appropriate paraphernalia in his many pockets when his body had been discovered fifteen days ago. Another birdwatcher had found it face down in the grove of white birches that filled the loop between the path that followed the edge of the bog and the one that forked to Ron's right. The body had escaped notice by birdwatcher traffic, concealed by the dense thicket of underbrush that lined both sides of the right path.

Homicide, the medical examiner had decreed. Dead at least two weeks and definitely not an accidental drowning. Not even a drowning. The body had certainly been soaked at some point; in fact a waterlogged *Petersen's Field Guide*, a jackknife, and a buckle from a binocular strap had been found in the lake in ankle-deep water, but death had been caused by trauma, namely a blow to the back of the head.

In Ron's opinion, the blow had been delivered by Jos Poot's wife, Orma, but it was an opinion his colleagues did not share. True, they acknowledged, Poot had been a cruel man. No less than three convictions of abuse, so the lady had motive. And true, Mrs. Poot was seen going into the park with her husband about a month ago — the same time he was reported missing — so she had opportunity. But how, Ron's colleague's argued, could such a tiny lady, a mere wisp really, dispatch her 250-pound husband on the head, admittedly from behind, while they were standing in the lake, and then lug him all the way to where the body was found?

A sharp ratatat-tat made Ron look up sharply. He leaned

back a bit. From the end of the birch grove, where the looping path rejoined the bogside one at the base of the Torrent, the sound came again. "Woodpecker," he declared, blinking rapidly against the low sun. "A Downy? No. Ah, it's a sapsucker!" he said, pleased with his identification.

"Enough birding." He squatted down one more time, this time bracing in advance for the cracking from his knees. "Better get more pictures," he said, fishing in his shirt pocket for fresh film. "Short of bringing them all out here, it's the only way I'll convince the doubters that the missus definitely bonked him. They'd only scare the birds anyway."

What argument will Ron Minaker use to explain to his colleagues how Mrs. Poot got the body to its point of discovery?

38

Two Embassy Cars
Are Missing

IT NEVER JUST RAINS. Not on this job. I got half a county of
empty back roads, two cars to look for, and one helicopter.

"Captain? Captain Surette? I think I see his, like, cell
phone? Down in the ditch? It's like really smashed?"

And the only officer around to help me is a rookie who
speaks in the comparative interrogative.

"Should I, like, go down and get it?"

Why me? First day this spring we've had a west wind hold
all day. I could have gone sailing. Well, I'm not going to rush.
When cops rush, they screw up. One thing. They're embassy
cars. Got to be the only two stretch Cadillacs in Dufferin
County. Unless they're ditched by now. That sun feels so
good on the back of my neck I hate to move. God, it's been
a long winter.

"Might be a clue to what happened to them? Like, the auxiliary troopers, I mean."

Almost forgot the troopers. Why did this have to happen
on my watch? The only witnesses and they're both missing.
So much for auxiliaries.

"Captain Surette! The phone? Like, the cell phone?"

"Yes, Constable, er, Oldchurch. Go down and get it."

If nothing else, it'll keep you busy so I can think. Let me see. According to our man here — our missing man — we got two embassy cars down the road there approaching Checkpoint One like they're supposed to. They stop before the intersection. Let's see, that's a good half mile away. And our man calls in 'cause he thinks something's not kosher.

"Captain! The phone's like really in pieces down here!"

Then people get out of the car with the Sudanese flags. Carrying Uzis. They get into the car with the Egyptian flags. That's when the call ends. Probably the smashed phone explains —

"Do you want me to pick them up? The pieces? Like, in an evidence bag? I should get a picture first, shouldn't I?"

What I don't like is behind us, up the hill, Checkpoint Two calls to say the cars split off in opposite directions, but then her phone goes dead too! This really smells.

"I'm gonna get the camera outa the car. OK, Captain? Oh, look! Over there? Like, the helicopter? Here it comes! Which way yuh gonna send it? There can't be more than an hour of daylight left."

Yes, which way? Well, I'm sure both cars have something to offer, but since at least one of the auxiliaries had to be in cahoots, the car I'd most like to find is the one with the Sudanese flags on the front fenders.

"You wouldn't be able, by any chance, er, Constable Oldchurch, to describe the flag of Sudan, would you?"

"Sudan. That's in, like, Africa, isn't it? Or is it Asia?"

Aside from the fact that the auxiliaries are missing, what has convinced Captain Surette that at least one of them is cooperating with the people in the missing embassy cars?

39

A Most
Confusing Robbery

ALTHOUGH SHE WAS PERFECTLY AWARE how important the trails of spattered blood were to the case, Detective-Inspector Mary-Joan Westlake had difficulty paying attention to the earnest explanations of the FOS.

"This spot here," the First Officer on the Scene was saying, pointing to dried droplets of blood on the concrete, "it's the start of the track for one of the suspects. Now see? Four, five yards down the alley here is the next one. Pretty consistent like this until you get to the dumpster around the corner. Now if . . ."

Some time later, before she could sign off, Mary-Joan had to ask the officer to go through it all again, just to be sure. The problem the first time was that the words of the store owner kept intruding on her consciousness.

"He wuz 'cross th' street 'afore I got off m' first shot," the old man had cackled with undisguised glee. "Y'see, she's allus cocked kinda slow till yuh get off the first round. That seems t' loosen 'er up." He held up a .45 Navy Colt that in all likelihood was as advanced in age as he was. "Too bad he wuz 'cross the street b' then. Took off runnin' down th' alley.

Mighta caught 'im otherwise 'n' finished the job!"

The words, the attitude, even the man's satisfaction at foiling the robbery attempt and successfully plunking the robber — these were things she'd heard all too often before. But this time it was special. Mary-Joan Westlake had grown up on this street when it was a place where people sat on porch stoops after supper to watch their kids play catch, where young couples strolled on the sidewalk holding hands while old men leaned on the store fronts and watched them with knowing expressions. It was a place where she would run to Mr. Evers's grocery store at seconds before six to buy a quarter pound of butter, and where Mr. Evers would hold off locking up because he saw her coming.

That neighborhood was gone now, along with Mr. Evers and his way of doing business. Replaced by things like the city-sponsored clinic that handed out hypodermic needles, and X-rated video stores where the owner kept a loaded .45 Colt under the cash drawer. Mary-Joan knew all about that of course, better than most quite likely, but she was never able to come here now without experiencing profound culture shock.

"The other suspect's trail starts in the same spot but across the alley." The FOS was still talking. "This is probably where the bullet hit. See the blood right there. Then . . ." He took a step. "Second one." A few more steps. "Third one here, and so on down to where you see those oil barrels. Suspect was in behind them."

Mary-Joan finally dragged her consciousness into the present.

"And you found them both on your first sweep?" she asked. "One by the dumpster, the other by those barrels? That's only about a hundred feet apart."

"It wasn't hard, Inspector," the officer replied. "When we got the 9-1-1 call, we were parked only a block away. Heck, in the summertime with the windows open, we'd have probably heard the shots. Besides, with those wounds they really weren't going to go far. The big problem is which one of them is the robber. The old guy at the video store sure isn't much help. All he can say is that the robber was average height and weight and wore a blue parka and a dark ski mask. Dark eyes, he's sure of that. Voice? Well, the robber didn't say anything. Really, all that old guy cares about is that whoever it was is carrying a .45 caliber slug. I don't think he even knows he winged two people."

Mary-Joan looked down the alley and then back at the video store. The waning evening light was reflecting off the windows, and were it not for the steel security bars behind them, she realized, it would have been easy to start thinking about Mr. Evers again. Instead, she grimaced and said to the FOS, "I've seen enough. You've done a good job here. I'm going to write you a positive for your file. Now . . ." She motioned to the officer to follow her. "Let's go back to the hospital and arrest the one you got at the dumpster."

"To the hospital," the policeman echoed. He started to ask a question but then thought better of it. Maybe at the hospital he'd have the answer, for at this very moment the two suspects were lying there in some discomfort on emergency ward gurneys. Both had bullet wounds estimated by the medical staff to be at best a couple of hours old, wounds that were made by a large caliber bullet.

Suspect One lay on a gurney in one of the examination rooms, his leg wrapped at the fleshy part of the calf. Suspect Two moaned about her shoulder wound from a gurney out in the hall of the overcrowded ward. Both were street people, their dark eyes red-rimmed from poor diet, lack of sleep, and, in all likelihood, drugs.

Suspect Two's story was that she was standing in the alleyway across the street from the video store when she heard a shout and looked up to see someone coming across the street toward her. She didn't see anyone shoot. Just heard a shot and then, from behind her, the sound of a ricochet. That's when she felt the hit in the back of her shoulder. After the second shot, she said, she wasn't about to wait around. She vaguely remembered running down the alley before she passed out.

Suspect One's account had no details at all. According to his version he had just stepped into the alley when he heard two shots. One of them hit him, he didn't know which. He didn't remember much of anything after that. Just wanting to get out of there as fast as possible and then waking up in the hospital.

Both suspects — somehow Mary-Joan knew this would be the case even before she asked — had blue parkas: standard issue from the neighborhood hostel.

Which of the two suspects is Mary-Joan Westlake going to arrest?

40

Transcript
(Copy #1 of 4)

PORT CREDIT, 28 MAY 1941
Inquiry into the Collision of the O.M.S. Oliver Mowat
and private vessel, "Gadabout" *

MAE APPLETON-NAIRN, CHAIR

APPLETON-NAIRN: Good morning. This inquiry is now on
the record. We are here to investigate the collision of the
O.M.S. Oliver Mowat and a private vessel, the, the (unintelli-
gible), yes, the Gadabout, on 30 September 1940. My name is
Mae Appleton-Nairn and I head the Investigative Branch of
the Department of Transport. Is there anyone who wishes to
be identified for the record?

ST. CLAIR: Oakwood St. Clair, Madam Chair, representing
the Port Authority.

---

* For specifications re both vehicles see Marine Registry File 498761HC.
See also Appendix to Report 12-A, 1940, of the Port Authority.

HAGEMAN: Callan Hageman, Madam Chair, representing Captain Ralph Ransom.

FLECK: Stephen Fleck, Madam Chair, representing Brewster and Zonka.

APPLETON-NAIRN: Who's . . . ? Oh yes, that's the owner of the private vessel. Is that a company?

FLECK: An incorporated entity, Madam Chair. I have copies of all the appropriate registrations.

APPLETON-NAIRN: Very well, thanks. Anyone else? Fine. Now, before we begin, may I remind everyone that this is an inquiry only, not a trial. My recommendations will go forward as to whether or not there is fault to be assessed in this collision, and whether or not charges will be laid. Are there any questions? Very good. Miss Clarke, would you come forward, please? Miss Carolyn Clarke is an officer with the Port Credit Marine Unit. Excuse me, Miss Clarke. This may be an appropriate moment to remind everyone that brevity and succinctness will be very much appreciated throughout this hearing. Have I made that clear? Good. Very well, Miss Clarke, you may proceed. Everyone has received a copy of your report, so I believe that all you need do is provide us with a very brief oral summary.

CLARKE: The Gadabout ran into the stern of the Oliver Mowat.

APPLETON-NAIRN: Actually, Miss Clarke, I didn't mean quite that brief. Perhaps, for the record, you could establish the situation, the time frame, and sequence of events? Maybe tell us about the ships? Flesh it out a wee bit.

CLARKE: The O.M.S. Oliver Mowat is a 32-meter double-ended R-O-R-O ferry —

APPLETON-NAIRN: R-O-R-O?

CLARKE: Roll-On-Roll-Off. Cars. They drive in one end and out the other.

APPLETON-NAIRN: I see.

CLARKE: Anyway, she's an R-O-R-O with three decks, bottom for cars, middle for passengers. Top deck is crew-only with duplicate wheelhouses bow and stern. The "Ollie" — that's her running name — makes 18 round trips a day across the Port Credit harbor to Mississauga Island. Leaves the city on the hour and the island on the half. Sailing time one way is 17 minutes. The Gadabout is a 9.7-meter pleasure yacht converted to a single covered deck, with a one-man control cab forward. Licensed for harbor cruises and private parties. On September 30th last year . . . Should I go on?

APPLETON-NAIRN: Please.

CLARKE: Eight minutes out on the return leg, the Mowat's entire lighting system failed. While she was dark the Gadabout ran into her stern. No damage to the ferry or injuries to passengers or crew. One death and seven injuries on the private boat. She sank.

APPLETON-NAIRN: The ferry can transport several hundred passengers, according to your report, Miss Clarke, and the group on the . . . the . . . Gadabout that night numbered fifteen. But your report stipulates there are no witnesses. Any chance your subsequent investigations have —

CLARKE: No.

APPLETON-NAIRN: That seems so unlikely —

CLARKE: Week night. Middle of the harbor. Heavy rain. Private vessel was totally enclosed except for the skipper forward. He's the fatality.

FLECK: I have a question, Madam Chair.

APPLETON-NAIRN: Go ahead, Mr. Fleck.

FLECK: Miss Clarke, your report does not give us the number of passengers on the Oliver Mowat. Why is that?

CLARKE: It wasn't available.

FLECK: Not available? That doesn't make —

CLARKE: Passengers board through a turnstile counter, but it wasn't operative on that crossing.

FLECK: Can you tell us why?

APPLETON-NAIRN: I think we'll wait for Captain Ransom on that one, Mr. Fleck. Do you have any more questions?

FLECK: Well, yes, one more. I have information — it does not appear in your report — that exactly two weeks before this collision, the same lighting blackout occurred on another Port Authority ferry, the James Whitney. Are you aware of this incident?

CLARKE: Yes.

FLECK: In your experience, Miss Clarke, is it normal for ships like the James Whitney and the Oliver Mowat to suddenly lose their lighting systems and go dark?

APPLETON-NAIRN: Mr. Fleck, you know better! This is an inquiry. Not the place for cross-examination. Now if you have no more questions, does anyone else . . . OK, Mr. St. Clair.

ST. CLAIR: The Oliver Mowat, Miss Clarke, and the James Whitney — these incidents with their lighting failures, could you tell us what steps the Port Authority took after the first occurrence?

CLARKE: The Whitney was found to have a faulty circuit breaker. This breaker was immediately replaced with another type of breaker in the Whitney and all the other ferries too.

ST. CLAIR: That would include the Oliver Mowat?

CLARKE: Yes.

ST. CLAIR: According to your report, no reason has yet been found to account for the Oliver Mowat's sudden blackout on September 30, is that correct?

CLARKE: Yes.

ST. CLAIR: But certainly one could not accuse the Port Authority of faulty maintenance practices, could one?

APPLETON-NAIRN: Mr. St. Clair! You're way over the line!

ST. CLAIR: I apologize, Madam Chair. Let me approach factually here, please. Miss Clarke, the two ferries in question, they are not the only ones run by the Port Authority, are they?

CLARKE: There are five altogether. All running run out of the same dock as the Mowat, between the city and the islands. All in service daily except for November to March.

ST. CLAIR: And it's my understanding that these ships are inspected regularly, including their electrical systems, by the Port Credit Marine Unit?

CLARKE: Twice a week in high season. Before the first outbound at 6 a.m. Once a week otherwise.

ST. CLAIR: High season begins . . . ?

CLARKE: First of May. Runs five months.

ST. CLAIR: Oh, one more thing. There are red and green — how can I describe them — clearance lights, or warning lights on the wheelhouses?

CLARKE: Yes. Red on the starboard and green to port. Oh, sorry! The other way around.

ST. CLAIR: And these are on a separate circuit, aren't they? That is, their power source is independent of the interior lighting system, isn't it? By that I mean, if the main system fails, these lights don't necessarily go out.

CLARKE: That's right. And they're supposed to be checked too, every time a ship leaves the dock.

ST. CLAIR: For the record, Miss Clarke, the Port Credit Marine Unit, is it associated in any way with the Port Authority?

CLARKE: The Unit is independent. Federal. The Authority is city.

APPLETON-NAIRN: Finished, Mr. St. Clair? Thank you, Miss Clarke. We are probably done, but please don't leave, just in case. Captain Ransom, would you come forward please? According to Miss Clarke's report, you were in command of the Oliver Mowat at the time of the collision?

RANSOM: That's right.

APPLETON-NAIRN: And you were in the wheelhouse at the time of the collision?

RANSOM: With the helmsman. That's regulation.

APPLETON-NAIRN: And according to what you told the Marine Unit, the collision occurred entirely without warning?

RANSOM: Like you said, I was in the wheelhouse. The Gadabout rammed our stern.

FLECK: Madam Chair!

APPLETON-NAIRN: No need, Mr. Fleck. Captain Ransom, I think it would be better if you avoided terms like "rammed" until it's established as appropriate, assuming it will be. I have one more question. On the 30th, were you in command all day?

RANSOM: No. See, the way it works is there's three watches, divided evenly. I was third watch that day.

APPLETON-NAIRN: Very well. No, don't step down. I'm sure there are more questions. All right, go ahead, Mr. Fleck.

FLECK: Thank you, Madam Chair. Now Captain Ransom, this inquiry has already heard about the lighting failures on Port Authority ferries, especially the crucial one on your ship on September 30. You acknowledge that these occurred, don't you?

RANSOM: Yes.

FLECK: And we have already heard from Miss Clarke about the red-green lighting system. Do you have anything to add to what she said?

RANSOM: No.

FLECK: Madam Chair, for the record, when — I'm sorry, if — if this case goes to trial, my client, Brewster and Zonka, will be contending that the Oliver Mowat's green-red system had failed along with the main system just prior to the collision.

APPLETON-NAIRN: It's on the record, Mr. Fleck. Continue.

RANSOM: Look, before you ask, I inspect those marker lights personally, outbound and inbound, before we cast off. They've never failed on any ship, ever, no matter what else has happened. Not in the 23 years I've been with the Authority.

FLECK: I see, Captain. Perhaps we can look at something else just for a minute then. The turnstile that counts the number of passengers, it wasn't working. Do you inspect that too?

RANSOM: Look, it was raining. Started to rain on my third trip and, you know, it rained steady into the next day. Anyway, there was only a handful of passengers and that Mississauga dock's got no cover. Now if they have to line up to go through the turnstile, it takes a while and they get soaked. So I disconnected it. The turnstile.

FLECK: Is there a chance, Captain Ransom, that because of the rain you might have skipped the light check too?

APPLETON-NAIRN: Mr. Fleck, I can appreciate your need to argue on behalf of your client, but once again, this is an inquiry. It's not an occasion for cross-examination.

FLECK: That's all my questions in any case, Madam Chair.

APPLETON-NAIRN: It's not my intent to call more witnesses at this time. Are there any other questions of Captain Ransom? Mr. St. Clair? No? What about you, Mr. Hageman? We haven't heard from you at all.

HAGEMAN: Normally, Madam Chair, I might have questions, but I believe that in an inquiry established to ascertain fault, I think we have heard enough to conclude that the Gadabout should certainly have been able to avoid colliding with this ferry.

APPLETON-NAIRN: I'm inclined to agree, Mr. Hageman, and my assessment of fault will reflect that.

Why should the Gadabout *have been able to avoid running into the stern of the* Oliver Mowat?

Solutions

1
The Body on Blanchard Beach

Dexter Treble explained that although the tire tracks were clear and preserved, there were no footprints. Had the body been brought to Blanchard Beach in the trunk of a car, or the back of a pickup truck, the deliverer would have had to get out of the car and walk around to the back to remove the body.

2
Esty Wills Prepares for a Business Trip

Sean wears an overcoat and there is snow, so it's winter in Chicago. While Paraguay's climate may not be well known (it's generally tropical), what is well known is that the country is situated below the equator, and therefore it's summer there. That being the case, why is Wills packing a scarf, gloves, and wool socks?

Incidentally, Japan did undertake a mulberry bush experiment in the 1980s for silk production. It continues.

Flying time, Chicago to Buenos Aires via commercial airlines, is about sixteen hours. Flying to Asuncion adds two hours for time-zone changes.

3

The Case of
the Buckle File

Gibraltar is spelled Gibralter in both the letter from Audrey and the one from Irene. The coincidence is too strong for Christine Cooper, who feels that Audrey, whose body, unlike that of Ernie, was never found, may be involved in a scheme to collect insurance. Irene's (Audrey's?) mistake is that she misspells Gibraltar even though, supposedly, she has been living there.

4

While Little Harvey
Watched

Carson Wicksteed, according to Harvey's parents, has had a difficult time because of his brother. To some people, that would imply motive. Carson must also know what he's doing with a chain saw, especially if he's been making a living out of firewood as Little Harvey's father says.

The beech tree fell over intact during the storm, its roots still attached to the tree and, at one edge, still clinging to the ground. Unless a sawyer is deliberately trying to make the stump fall back into the hole, he will not cut away the upper part of the tree first, because it is the counterbalancing weight of the upper part that keeps the stump and root system from doing so. Since Carson is a professional, he would surely have known this.

5

The Murder of
Mr. Norbert Gray

The letters in the evidence bag are personal ones, mailed by someone. Mike Roslin tapped the stamps on both letters, so it is likely that whoever mailed the letters licked the stamps.

The saliva can be tested for DNA.

6

A Holdup at the
Adjala Building

The Adjala Building must function as an almost perfect mirror at almost any time of day, but especially before lunch on this bright day when there would be no direct sunlight on the copper-tinted plate glass doors. The courier quite certainly would have been able to see details about the thief in its reflection.

7

Filming at L'Hôtel du Roi

Before the twentieth century's popularization of efficient, lobbyless — and characterless –– hotels, the lobby of a grand hotel was designed to be part of the experience of a hotel stay, and it was usually quite a busy place. Therefore Charlotte's colliding with Van Slotin can be entirely natural, especially if the acting brings it off effectively, because there would be more than enough distractions and activities to make a collision like this legitimate.

What bothers Barney King is that the writers have made Charlotte too obvious with her bare hands. In the forties, a lady, even one with questionable intent, would never have entered the lobby of a grand hotel without hat and gloves. (Sy's marginal note makes this clear.) Charlotte has a hat, but when she adjusts the seams of her stockings, it's clear she does not have gloves on. Perhaps she needs bare hands to make the dip, but Barney wants the writers to come up with a better approach.

8

Whether or Not to Continue Up the Mountain

When Chris looked through the binoculars the first time and saw the cattle calmly chewing their cud, she also saw their ears twitching. The only reason an animal does that is to shoo away insects. If there are insects bothering the Swiss Browns up the mountainside, then it cannot be very cold.

9

Nothing Better than a Clear Alibi

Only Augusta and Siobhan can support the contention that they were in the hallway when the three shots were fired that apparently killed Siobhan's husband, Paisley. Everything else can be attested to by other tenants, the janitor, and Esther Goldblum.

Where Augusta Reinhold's account breaks down, and what makes Nik Hall suspicious of Siobhan's alibi, is Augusta's statement that after Esther left, she got dressed "as you see me now" and came down the elevator to Siobhan's floor. Nik realizes that without the help of Raythena, who does not appear until one, Augusta would never have been able to button the dress she has on, in the space of time described, because her hands are ravaged by arthritis. She could never have made it to the elevator and be in it with her granddaughter within the time she claims.

10

Guenther Hesch Didn't Call In!

If there are seventeen filters in the bowl, Guenther has lit twenty-two cigarettes, the first one according to habit at eight o'clock and the rest on the quarter hour thereafter. The first four, producing four filters and four butts, would have been lit at 8 A.M., 8:15, 8:30, and 8:45. The fifth cigarette, lit at

9 A.M., would have been rolled from the butts of the previous four. Continuing in this way, Guenther would have snapped three more filters and lit up at 9:15, 9:30, and 9:45. The three butts from these, along with the roll-your-own butt from 9 A.M., would have produced a roll-your-own cigarette for 10 A.M. In this fashion Guenther would have produced three more filters by 11 A.M., at which time he'd have four more butts for another roll-your-own, then three more filters by noon and three more by 1 P.M.

Since there are seventeen filters in the bowl, and one butt (from the 1 P.M. roll-your-own), Guenther must still have been in the room at 1:15, when he broke off the seventeenth filter and lit up.

11

Right Over the
Edge of Old Baldy

When Pam heard the scream, she was only a minute or so away from the edge of Old Baldy. She had been proceeding up the Bruce Trail from Kimberley Rock. Hadley Withrop said that he and Sheena had eaten lunch at Kimberley Rock and had been at the edge of Old Baldy for only two minutes when Sheena went over. If this account is true, then the Withrops had gone up the trail just ahead of Pam. By the same token, if that fact is true, the Withrops would have taken out the spiderweb that Pam ran into. There would not have been sufficient time for the spider to rebuild. If the Withrops had not come up the trail ahead of Pam, why does he say that?

12
Sunstroke, and
Who Knows What Else!

Evan is duplicating the position in which Cadet Elayna was tied to stakes, and is doing so in precisely the same place, with the stakes reinserted into the same holes. If Evan can use a shadow from the stake to keep the sun out of his eyes, the stakes must be angled toward him.

Basic laws of physics tell us that stakes angled away from him would be hard to pull out. Not so if the stakes are angled toward him. Cadet Elayna could have pulled out the stakes if he'd wished to.

13
Should the Third
Secretary Sign?

Probably not, for the photograph is fraudulent. Russia uses the Cyrillic alphabet, in which the letters of Lenin's name, most particularly the "L" and "I," bear no resemblance at all to those letters as we know them in the modern Roman alphabet.

The Cyrillic alphabet, modified from Greek by St. Cyril (c. 827–869), is used for Slavonic languages like Russian and Bulgarian. As Third Secretary, Ena would surely have known that, and likely would have declined to sign.

When the USSR moved into Czechoslovakia on August 21, 1968, Austria became the first stop for most refugees.

Lenin died in 1924. In 1930 his tomb was built in Red

Square, with his embalmed body visible behind glass. It became a type of shrine in Moscow but was removed after perestroika.

14

A Successful Bust at 51 Rosehill

The townhouses at Woodington Manor are all the same size and shape. And the interiors are also designed so that each story is the same size and shape. Jack Atkin has determined that Number 51 must have a false wall, because the basement window wall — the wall facing west — is not the same length as the west wall on the first floor. The first floor has the same furniture pieces as the basement, but with lamps on end tables. In the basement, as Mandy Leamington describes it, the two massage chairs are jammed in between the sofa and the wall.

How much he was influenced by the geraniums is moot, but as an aficionado of this flower, Jack certainly would not ignore the fact that there are six on the first floor and five in the basement. That discrepancy likely led to further analysis.

15

The Case of the Body in Cubicle 12

In a "sweatshop" environment, where everything is high-tech and geared to achieve maximum production, this woman's cubicle has a fountain pen in it. Given that there is also a bottle of ink (taking up valuable space along with a desk lamp), she must have been exercising at least some mild defiance of her sterile working conditions; i.e., she must have actually *used* the fountain pen. For something as personal and final as her own final note, this woman in particular would not have been likely to use the printer.

16
The Case of the Broken Lawnmower

The rectangle Kristy painted marks the only spot on the mower's front lawn from where he can see across the street into the alley. It also marks the spot where the nut was found, and where the witness says his lawnmower handle came apart, causing him to turn off the mower and then look up to witness the shooting. However, the two investigators found the bolt five or six steps away. It is at this point where the lawnmower handle would have come apart. Even if the nut falls off a bolt, the structure will hold together, however loosely, until the bolt, no longer secured, comes out. Then the handle will come apart.

17
A Quiet Night with Danielle Steel?

The platform jutting out from the side of the Jacuzzi is completely clean. If the victim had taken a novel and a drink to the tub, and if the drink was almost entirely consumed, then the glass would have been lifted up and set down several times, leaving round marks on the surface of the platform. If she died of natural causes and then sank into the water, taking the novel in with her, those marks would still be there. Even an obsessively neat woman would not have wiped them after each sip. (Besides, the only cloth, the face cloth, was untouched.) Someone must have cleaned too thoroughly in an attempt to rid the place of evidence.

18

Vandalism at the Bel Monte Gallery

While Robbie paced on the sidewalk, waiting for Patchy, Dale stood between the sidewalk and the Bel Monte Gallery, under a mature chestnut tree. The time is just before Christmas, and there would not be any leaves on the tree. Four months ago, when the paintings were slashed, the tree would have been in full leaf. That it is a chestnut tree is not overly significant; however, the leaves of this type of tree are very large and the tree always leafs very fully.

From the bus shelter, Patchy draws the attention of the two investigators to the window "right b'tween them branches there." His ability to "witness" would almost certainly have been thwarted by the leaves at that time.

19
Laying Charges Too Quickly?

Special Investigator Hope Rogers believes, at least at this stage, that someone is trying to set up Nunzio by planting the apparent murder weapon in his tool box. She suspects it is a plant because Nunzio Scalabianca is a craftsman, an artist in his ornamental metalwork trade. Until she can investigate further, it's far safer to assume that a true craftsman would never have a cheap tool in his own cache of equipment. A craftsman would use only quality equipment.

20
Taking Down the Yellow Tape

When he came in the driveway and got out of his car, Geoffrey noted the garbage strewn about by the raccoons and saw dog-food cans. It's very unlikely that a stranger would be able to come in to Dietrich Lindenmacher's home at night and kill the victim in his bed, if the victim had a dog. The dog would surely have roused Lindenmacher to the point where he'd have gotten out of bed. And, if Lindenmacher had a burglar alarm system, it is equally unlikely that he would have been the type of person to treat the dog's barking casually.

Although the matter of the dog is itself enough to arouse second thoughts, the burglar alarm offers technical information too. All but the most primitive alarm systems are designed to go off if their circuit is cut. But it is possible to "jump" the circuit, rewire it so that the electricity bypasses the system. To do that, one needs to know where the alarm circuit is connected, and it's not likely that a stranger would know that.

At the very least, this suspect deserves a second look, either because he is innocent or because he is not a stranger.

21
Problem-Solving in Accident Reconstruction 101

Turtles do cross roads from one habitat to another, usually following some territorial imperative or breeding instinct. This happens particularly in the setting here, where the road has apparently created two separate swamps. And turtles do grow large enough to be a potential problem for car drivers.

In this case, the weakness of the driver's story is the place where she reports the turtle: at the top of the hill. Turtles — in fact all members of the order Chelonia — are not celebrated for either their logic or their adventurousness. Even so, for one to go up a hill, away from its natural habitat on either side, is unlikely in the extreme.

22
Before the First
Commercial Break

It is too obvious that Katzmann is lying. The allegedly dropped-in-panic revolver is in front of, and against, a door that swings inward (Gilhooley fingers the barrel of the middle hinge). The alleged robber could not have left it like that and then opened the door to flee, because opening the door would have knocked the revolver away.

23
More than One
St. Plouffe?

Alfred-Louis St. Plouffe Junior fils.

The confession is written in grammatically impeccable prose. The same quality applies to the speech of the younger St. Plouffe Junior. The speech of the elder St. Plouffe Junior, however, while grammatically elegant for the most part, has some awkward errors, suggesting he does not have quite the grammatical exactitude necessary to write the confession in the way it was offered.

The elder St. Plouffe says adverse when averse is the correct choice, and previous instead of prior. Further, he says *between my son and myself*, a very popular vulgarism, instead of *between my son and me*. The use of excepting over except is another grammatical sin.

24
When the Oxygen Ran Out

Either there is a series of genuine and unfortunate coincidences or there is a conspiracy that has led to the death of Humbert Latham.

The day nurse may have left innocently; after all, she had arranged to leave early. The valet's accident may have been real, along with the subsequent wooziness and inability to speak. As for the night nurse, we don't know why she failed to show up, but if the other two were legitimately absent, she could have been too. On the other hand, if there is a conspiracy by one or two or all three of the above, the security guard, if he was the regular patroller, would likely have been part of it.

Fran noted that the lamp was on in the room with Latham's body. If, as Sergeant Hong ordered, nothing was to be touched, then it must have been on all night. Since there was no blind or curtain over the window, the regular patroller would have noted the light, and unless he was in on a plot, would surely have investigated.

25

The Terrorist in Fountain Square

Number Four, the painter. With the information Connie has, it's a judgment call; all she knows is that one of them has the switch. With the exception of the painter, each has at least a legitimate claim to be in the square. Number Four, however, in this place of aluminum and brick and glass, has nothing to paint.

26

A Matter of Balance

Tom Jones knows his interview was a set-up because the man presenting himself as Agent Bronowski would not have made the height prerequisites to be an agent of the FBI. Although few police forces would dare to enforce height or gender or ethnic restrictions today, it was fairly common at the time Tom Jones had his meeting.

We know Tom is not tall because in the elevator he is careful not to let his face get too close to the marine lieutenant's dandruff-covered shoulder blade. Yet Tom, sitting on the same type of chair as Bronowski, is able to study a birthmark on the alleged agent's scalp, suggesting that Bronowski is even shorter than he.

That the story takes place at a time when height restrictions were enforced is confirmed by the fact that it is just prior to World War II. To be precise, the date is October 30, 1938, the Sunday night before Hallowe'en when Orson Welles's Mercury Theatre presented its adaptation of H. G. Wells's *The War of the Worlds*.

Polyesters were introduced to the world in 1940.

27
Paying Attention to Esme Quartz

Esme's one friend is her dog. This is a city neighborhood where dogs cannot roam free but must be walked. It had been raining for a day and a half and the dog, for biological cum hygienic reasons, had to be walked, rain or shine. The dog hair on Esme's coat told MaryPat that Esme had a genuine reason to be on the street in the rain, and since her walking-in-the-rain style would have been naturally different from the style of other pedestrians because of the dog, it is quite reasonable to believe that she had a good look at the shooter. That Esme actually knew the shooter was a bonus.

28

Investigating the Failed Drug Bust

Officer Dana is already under quiet investigation; that is a given. The second officer to be checked out now is the narcotics squad officer from Gallenkirk Park. He is the one who said that the approaching wino (Officer Dana) could be heard walking through the leaves.

Quite clearly, the time is early spring. There is some snow still remaining in shaded spots and in the lee of tree trunks. Betty Stadler is sure she noticed a robin and remarks that it is an early returner. In early spring, the millions of leaves that fell from the many trees in Gallenkirk Park the previous fall will be soggy and compressed and matted together. This would have been especially so at the time of the failed drug bust and during Betty's subsequent investigation because the effect of the melted snow has been compounded by several days of drizzle.

For Officer Dana to have made noise walking through the leaves, he would have had to stir up the surface very deliberately, implying some connection to the meeting of drug dealers about to take place. Another possibility is that the narcotics officer is not telling the truth about the way Officer Dana approached. Still a third is that the two officers are in this together. Thus, for the moment at least, Lieutenant Stadler has two police officers to investigate.

29
A Surprise Witness for the Highland Press Case

In his "favorite" pub, as he claims The Toby Jug to be, Wally Birks is not going to stop at the entrance to the washroom alcove to orient himself on the direction of the "Gents." He'd know which way to turn from habit.

30
The Last Will and Testament of Albion Mulmur

The poet in Kay makes her sensitive to the way Regina Mulmur treats the harness shop. If Regina had "almost used to live in here" as a little kid, she would surely have been more sensitive to the place than she was.

By itself, however, that is not enough. The convincing clue is the way in which Regina closed the door. She seemed to know instinctively that it needed a good shove to close it because the hinges were worn. If she hadn't been here in twenty years, as she says, then it's not likely she'd have known that. Since the will benefiting her was found here, it's fairly clear to Kay that Regina had paid the shop a recent visit.

31
What Happens in Scene Three?

It should be reasonably straightforward to conclude that the gunman's fingerprints are now in George Fewster's safe — on the Peacock egg. If George were to be dispatched, as the contract apparently dictates, the safe would surely be opened and the identity of the gunman placed at risk of being revealed. On the other hand, if the gunman does not shoot him, George can simply give the egg and fingerprints to the police at will.

But there is a quid pro quo. If the partner "cannot afford to let George live," he will surely try this again. Thus, if the gunman was to turn his professional skills against the man who hired him in the first place, that danger to George would be removed. At the same time, by doing that, he ensures George's silence, since even though George has not committed any crime by turning his partner's plan back on himself, it would be impossible for George to offer the police some fingerprints without arousing suspicion and provoking investigations.

32
Almost an Ideal
Spot for Breakfast

If the house has been empty for the past week while the Melches were in Nassau, the large leaves on the plants facing the east window would have rotated naturally toward the light, i.e., the window, over this period of time, particularly in winter. But the leaves were turned toward the west wall. (As he stood in the doorway, Laurie noticed them turned toward him.) Someone who cares for plants had rotated them — standard procedure in indoor plant care — very recently. Laurie Silverberg assumes, quite logically, that a break-and-enter perpetrator is not likely to have done this. That leaves one very likely suspect.

33
Investigating the Explosion

Because the blast came from inside the house. It must have been set up to look like "Nazi types" were responsible.

Doug Doyle's clue comes from the direction of the swastika and the smear from the sprinkler system. Although swastikas can go both clockwise and counterclockwise, as Doug pointed out, the Nazi party in Germany chose a clockwise rotation. Therefore, if a swastika were to be applied to the inside of a glass door in order to appear as though it had been put on from the outside, the artist (terrorist?) would have done it counterclockwise.

Granted, a careful investigation would certainly reveal which side of the glass held the symbol. However, Marni says that "on first impression" it appears some Nazi types were involved, and that may be all the bombsetter wanted to do. Besides, if the door were sufficiently shattered, a less than utterly precise examination might miss the fact.

Where the scheme broke down was in the smearing by the sprinkler system. The sprinklers must be inside of course, and would have come on after the blast. If the water fell on the markings and smeared them, the door would have to have been blasted outward. That is why Doug is suspicious.

34

Some Uncertainty about the Call at 291 Bristol

Shaun's maternal instincts are readily apparent, so it must seem strange, at the very least, that Paige's parents would go away, leaving her alone in the house, with the burglar alarm not working, especially given the recent stalking incident on the campus.

Moreover, if the man in black was breaking and entering, it seems highly unlikely he would wear jewelry that might jingle.

The strongest doubt of all, though, originates from Paige. If she had just emerged from the shower, the mirror in which she claims to have seen the man in black would have been fogged with vapor.

35

The Case of the Missing Child

While standing in the doorway, Audrey noticed that, behind the father, the venetian blinds are open. At the other window, the mother is looking out. Both say they have not been in the room since Lexie was put to bed last night. In a bedroom exposed to higher buildings such as the neighboring apartments, it surely would have been natural to draw the blinds. This is especially so in light of the mother's statement that anything, including light, can set Lexie off. It seems the parents have much more explaining to do.

36

A Clever Solution
at the County Fair

The obvious, in the case of homing pigeons: Pincher will have to take the first-prize ribbon off, and then have the judges make their decision again. He will then release the winners of the first prize. Since they are homing pigeons, they will fly home — either to Maxwell Stipple's cote or to Madonna Two Feather's.

37

Even Birdwatchers Need
to Watch Their Backs

The scene Ron sees consists of a path on his left at the edge of McCarston's Lake and one that forks to his right. And, he can see where the two paths rejoin at the foot of the Devil's Torrent.

The path on the right must be the one that hikers and bird-watchers use to go around the lake when there is more water in it (and when the Devil's Torrent really deserves its name).

When the weather turns drier and the lake shrinks in size owing to less water flow, another path will develop because birdwatchers especially will stay to the water's edge where the birds are.

If Jos Poot was killed earlier in the season, and in the water, as is apparently the case, Mrs. Poot could have used water buoyancy to get his body to its hiding place.

38

Two Embassy Cars Are Missing

Captain Surette enjoys the sun on the back of his neck as he looks down the road to where the embassy cars stopped at the intersection. Since there's only an hour of daylight left, he's looking east. There has been a west wind all day. As embassy cars come toward one, it is only possible to see the front edges of the flags mounted on the front fenders because of the air motion. Even when they stopped, the west wind would have held the flags that way. The first auxiliary trooper, therefore, would not have been able to distinguish which car was flying which flag, and since his report does that, the captain draws an obvious conclusion.

Captain Surette would prefer to locate the car with Sudanese flags first, because the trooper's report implied that the Egyptian one was the principal vehicle. Since there is collusion in this case, the Captain interprets that as a deliberate attempt to mislead pursuers, so he is opting for the opposite.

The Sudanese flag, incidentally, is three horizontal stripes, red (top), white, and black, with a green triangle based on the hoist. Egypt's flag is similarly striped, but with the national emblem center, in gold.

39

A Most Confusing Robbery

Since both suspects qualify, potentially, Mary-Joan has to rely on the video store owner's account. He said that the robber he shot "took off runnin'" down the alley. The droplets of blood that ended at the dumpster were quite widely spaced, four or five yards apart, the FOS had explained. The spacing would suggest someone who was able to run pretty fast.

The suspect hit in the leg, however, would not have been able to run as quickly, with the result that the droplets would be closer together. Therefore Mary-Joan Westlake is going to arrest Suspect Two, the one with the shoulder wound.

40
Transcript (Copy #1 of 4)

Captain Ransom had the third watch, which begins at 6 P.M. It started to rain on his third round trip (8 P.M.). The collision occurred on the next trip, eight minutes into the return leg from Mississauga Island (9:38 P.M.), so the accident occurred in darkness. However, any municipality that has five ferries running every hour (in high season) has to be a large one: a city. Since running time from Mississauga Island to the city dock is only 17 minutes, the lights of the city must be clearly visible to all inbound craft. If the *Gadabout* were being safely and responsibly handled, the outline of a ship the size of the O.M.S. *Oliver Mowat* would have been clearly detailed against the illumination from the city, and therefore avoidable, whether or not her clearance lights were working.